Elizabeth

High Priestess

Author Note

This is a fictional literary product of my imagination, for the most part. I have taken creative liberty, by incorporating information gathered from different sources, in the writing of this fiction. I am not promoting any form of religion nor am I making claims to be an expert in such matters.

David R McCovey

Prologue

=

From 1719 to 1731, the majority of slaves imported to the French colony of Louisiana came from West Africa, bringing with them their cultural practices, language, and religious beliefs.

Some religious philosophy is based on a belief in ancestral spirits and ancestor worship.

Through dance, music, singing, and the use of 'Zombi', another name for the Vodou snake, the connection to the spirits are achieved.

Unlike the images of Catholicism, 'Zombi' represents - healing, knowledge, and the connection between Heaven, and Earth.

These religious practices believe that ancestral spirits can intercede in the lives of Vodou followers.

The cultural practices and religion brought by Africans has adapted and combined with European Judeo-Christianity, and Roman Catholicism to form a distinctive Louisiana Vodou form of worship.

In the early 1700's Sanite' Dede became to be known as the Queen of Vodou in New Orleans.

Renowned for her 'Love Portions', Marie Laveau, a devout Catholic, became Queen of New Orleans Vodou when word of her powers, including performing exorcisms, spread throughout the city during the 1800"s.

Vodou queens became central figures in the United States in the early part of the nineteenth century. Queens presides over rituals and ceremonies, they provide charms, amulets, and cure ailments.

Queens also have been known to administer magical powders to destroy enemies or to attract lovers.

No one person has been recognized as Queen of Vodou in New Orleans since the death of Marie Laveau.

***

Dela Eden cried out in pain as the mid-wives was gathered around the hut, the birth was not going to be easy. The villagers of Zooti awaited the arrival of its newest member.

The heavy dark clouds of late December created a supernatural feeling as the rain felled, drenching the earth, bringing with it new birth.

Kwami, the father of the child, pacing nervously outside the birthing hut, was concern for his wife and their first child; he listened to Dela Eden cries.

Her cries were soon replaced by another cry, a cry of struggle for life that echoed throughout the village, and up to the heavens.

The Mother Queen, the elder of all females, took the child, washed her in the rain under the skies, and checked, counted; her limbs, fingers, and toes before laying the child in her mother's arms.

Late in the night, the rain had past; the Nganga who had prepared an amulet that would protect this girl child from evil spirits led the ritual ceremony.

The villagers danced to the beat of the drums as the Nganga called to the ancestral spirits to make their presence known.

Spiritual possession came over the people, the Nganga, in a trance, called out "this child speaks with God."

On the third day Kwami took the child into the jungle, held it up to the sky and pronounced, "Behold this girl child, she is called Binta."

I

Stale; that's how Nick described the air in this cheap hotel room at Dauphine Street and Orleans Avenue in the French Quarters of New Orleans.

The strong odor of urine dominated the aroma of the many scents that availed themselves to his senses.

The sound of Jazz hovered on the still humid air of the night.

In his room, with no air conditioning, Nick sat facing a noisy window fan as he try to cool his body as sweat ran down his cheek adding to the wetness of his already soaked shirt.

It was after midnight, the temperature was in the high 80"s. There were scores of people out on the street, party goers were in full swing.

Nick had attempted to sleep but the nightmares became to intense making sleeping difficult.

He has not had a descent night sleep in years; to many ghosts. Images of battles fought long ago haunted him still.

He could not help but to listen to the sounds coming from the room next to his.

The couple was in the middle, or at the end, of a violent sexual marathon. The woman was moaning, she was almost screaming with pleasure.

The bed was banging the wall and on top of it all was this heavy deep grunting. He tried to shift his focus when he felt himself getting aroused. He felt like a pervert, he checked his watch and noticed the time.

He slipped on his shoes; he had not like the ideal of walking on this dirty, and stained, carpet in his socks but the heat caused his feet to sweat.

Nick left the hotel, walked out into the night, and was immediately engulfed with the heat and humility of southern Louisiana in late, July.

He walked down Orleans Avenue, turned onto Bourbon Street, he stopped to orient himself taking mental note of the action on the street.

Across the street, in front of Fat Catz Music Club, a tap dancer entertained what Nick believed to be tourist.

Bourbon Street was boasting with activity, to include hustlers "of all types" drug dealers, gamblers, and sellers of flesh.

He walked a few block, 'down river', along Upper Bourbon Street and then entered Razzo Bar & Bistro.

***

A secret ritual in the swampland of Bayou St John took on a supernatural feeling as the rhythmic beat of dancing drums captivated the crowd as they swayed, and chanted as the spirits of the ancestors took hold of each person gathered.

September is the spiritual season of celebration and the transition into the Voodoo New Year.

The crowd was in a state of frantic spiritual possession as the drums beat got faster and louder.

From behind the bonfire, Binta stepped out into the open adorning the mask of the head female Gelede spirit, Lya Lase.

The light of the fire glittered off the sweat that ran down her naked body.

She was possessed, not by the ancestors but by the spirits of the Loa that she represents. She raised the sacrificial knife high over her head as she danced in tuned with the drumbeats.

Her eyes rolled back into her head, she was in a trance. She thrust the knife downward, it penetrated deep into the chest of the virgin sacrifice, and she drew out the heart.

Binta healed the warm heart over her head offering it to the Ancestors as blood ran down her arms, and dripped into her face.

The crowd became more excited, intoxicated, all started ripping off their clothes, as the rhythm of the drum remained constant.

The people filed by the sacrificial altar, dipped their hands into the blood of the young woman, and rubbed it over themselves.

Sexual tension was in the air, men and women, alike, became aroused. Bodies began to join, all was engaged, while Binta stood over the scene as her place as Queen has been consummated.

The body of the young victim was buried deep in the swamps she will never be spoken of. She now belongs to God.

Following the tradition of her ancestors, Lady Binta now sits as the Queen of New Orleans Voodoo.

Unlike the first Queen of Voodoo in New Orleans - Sanite' DeDe, or the famous, and longest reining queen - Marie Laveau. Lady Binta's roots traced back to the cradle of Voodoo.

***

"Calm down, young lady," Christina's mother playfully scorned her daughter as she continue to brush the sand and twigs out of Christina's hair.

Christina had been helping her father mend fishing nets when she decided to lie down in the sand; she began to daydream about America.

The only thing she knew of America is what she read in books and magazines. In addition, the many told over stories told by people who heard it told by someone else.

Her father had noticed that she had stopped engaging her chore. He did not mind, he would have been at sea today; but decided to mend his nets and make minor repairs to his boat at this time.

He had not wanted to be far from home so he could spend time with his daughter.

"Look at this one, all grown. Your mother tells me you are off to America." Christina's aunt said, as she came into the house interrupting Christina and her mother's conversation.

"Yes Auntie Carmella, I am going to America with Elizabeth and Joseph on vacation," Christina, who is normally shy and reserved, responded excitedly.

"America, ha! Not a good place too many Blacks and Mexicans. How can you allow this child to go off alone?" Carmella shouted.

"Carmella did you not hear Christina? She said that she will be with Elizabeth and Joseph" Lisola defended her daughter.

"That Elizabeth is a strange girl" Carmella interjected.

Christina and her mother knew of Carmella's tendency to speak ill of people and her effort to downplay other people aspirations. The two had seen her in action on many of occasions, and knew that it was a waste of time trying to win her approval.

The day before Christina was to leave for America, she and her family attended mass. The Roman Catholic Church has been a very important part of her life since birth.

Her home of Levanzo is a very beautiful small island of Sicily where the Roman Catholic Church is the religious authority.

Christina, with her mother and father, traveled to Rome to the home of her father's brother, and father to Elizabeth and Joseph, soon after Mass.

Elizabeth took Christina by the hand, they run off to Elizabeth's room soon after Christina, and her family arrived.

The two acted more like sisters when together, even though Elizabeth was four years older, they shared many secrets.

It was Elizabeth who convinced Joseph, who had just completed his studies at the university, to invite Christina to join them on their planned trip to America. Joseph had not shown any interest in Christina nor anyone on her side of the family.

His father had achieved a level of financial success as the owner of one of the largest auto dealerships in Rome. Christina's father was a fisherman and Joseph considered him a fool, but he loved his sister very much so he agreed to her request.

One secret that the two young women shared was Elizabeth fascination with the occult. In particular, Baphomet, described by scholars as an imagined pagan deity of Christian folklore that was revived in the 19th century.

"I have something to show you," Elizabeth proclaimed.

"What is it this time?" Christina asked.

"Will if you don't want to see it I will not show you. Miss Smarty," Elizabeth responded playfully.

Elizabeth went into her closet and came out with a circular tube approximately four feet long.

She opened it and revealed a poster on which contained the image of the Sabbatic Goat.

Christina was stunned, and a little frighten, she blessed herself with the sign of the cross.

"Why do you have that?" she asked.

"Relax its harmless," Elizabeth said, in a calm reassuring voice.

"But its Satan," Christina announced.

The image of the Sabbatic Goat stayed in Christina's mind, affecting her ability to sleep.

She said a number of silent prays to the mother of God throughout the night.

The next morning the three of them boarded a plane for America.

II

During the early 1970"s it was reported that the Marcello crime family still had influent over the political structure of New Orleans.

As a sign of respect, messenger delivered a communiqué to a Marcello family associate announcing the expected arrival of an associate of a friend from Villalba, Sicily on business to keep a promise.

And a request for the extension of assistance be granted.

***

Razzo's was buzzing with people, the sound of Frank Sinatra blared through the jukebox. The smell of fresh baked dread and garlic filled the air.

Nick stopped just inside the entry and scanned the faces of the people in the club before walking up to the bar and handing the bartender a business card.

The bartender looked at the card then looked at Nick, back at the card again. He stared at Nick for a long time before pointing to an office in the back of the club.

Nick turned in the direction the bartender pointed, he notice a big burly guy standing guard at the door.

The bartender signaled the guard; he gave way when Nick approached.

Nick entered a dimly lit room where three rough looking guys' seat at a round table. Each was engaging a plate of food, a full course meal was laid out on the table, and they all looked up in unison and stared at him.

The communiqué had spoke of Nick's un-usualness, but these three guys did not know if they could nor wanted to accept him as an Italian.

He had grown accustom to people staring as they try to figure out his ethnicity.

Nick had the facial features of his father, muscular with jet-black hair and hazel eyes that he inherited from his mother's people.

Cleo Nickelson was born Mohammad Ag-nello, a name given to him by his mother who was a member of the Kabyle people of Northern Africa. His father; he had not known but was told that he was an Italian.

His uncle told him that his father was operat-ing in Northern Africa as a member of the French Foreign Legion, where he meets his mother, and that he went by the name Frank Agnello.

Later Nick discovered that his father was born in Naples, Sicily.

At age, twenty-six, following in his father footsteps, Nick made his way from Africa to France were he swore his legions to the French Foreign Legion and legally changing his name.

He spent the next fifteen years with the Legion, and made a number of associations during that time.

Nick looked from one face to the other and notices that the three men had the same face; they were triplets.

"Nick" Nick introduced himself.

"That's Frank, Frank and I'm Frank," one of the guys answered as he pointed from one to the other.

"I'm supposed to see Frank about a package," Nick said.

"Over there, the envelope," one of the other Frank said as his pointed to the desk.

Nick walked over and picked up a large vanilla envelope, tucked it into his shirt, and walked out of Razzo's and headed back to the hotel.

***

After spending the first three days of their vacation sightseeing in New York and Washington DC, Christina, Elizabeth, and Joseph decided to fly to New Orleans.

After checking into the New Orleans International Hostel on Carondelet Street, the group makes their way to New Orleans downtown, then they went sightseeing in one of the famous cemeteries.

They attended midday mass at Saint Joseph's Catholic Church on Tulane Avenue, reportedly the largest church in New Orleans and build between 1869 and 1892.

Christina, been more intoned with the Roman Catholic Church in her home country, took note of the differences in the structure and formality of the service.

Along the Mississippi River the three visitors snapped photographs near Algiers Point, and then headed for the French Quarters; Bourbon Street.

The group emerged themselves in the favor and spirit of the Quarters, to include sampling in little crawfish.

Elizabeth noticed the sign when they passed the Ramada Hotel, The New Orleans Paranormal, and Occult Research Society was having their convention in the Banquet Room.

She felt herself been drawn to see what was happening inside.

Joseph did not want any part of it, his mind was on Jazz.

He had taken a music appreciation class while at the university and fail in love with the sounds of Louis Armstrong. He developed such a passion for Armstrong's music that he decided to take up the trumpet, and began to emulate Armstrong's style until he became a proficient trumpeter.

He sets out to take advantage of his time in New Orleans, he wanted to meet and possibly learn from fellow musicians.

He landed at the Howlin Wolf.

Jimmy Hicks, known around town as 'Little Mo', was on stage. Joseph, captivated by his sound, made his way to the stage to introduce himself to 'Little Mo' during intermission.

"Where you from?" Little Mo asked.

"Rome Italy" Joseph said.

"Never played Rome, you know Jazz?" Little Mo spoke as he tried to remember his past.

"Studied 'Satchmo' while in college" Joseph explained.

Little Mo shot a skeptical look at Joseph; he looked around and about, saw what he was looking for, picked up one of his back up trumpet and handed it to Joseph. Joseph took the horn, tested it, and then plays a small portion of Louis Armstrong's, 'Ain't MisBehavin'.

Little Mo, with a wide grin, slapped himself on the knee and proclaimed, "Son that was ok."

"You come back tomorrow and sit in during the first show" Little Mo invited.

Joseph was walking on air when he returned to the lobby of the Ramada Hotel to meet Elizabeth and Christina as planned.

Christina blessed herself with the sign of the cross and gives a private thinks to god when she saw Joseph entered the lobby.

Joseph noticed that she was upset and anxious.

Christina is a devoted Christian; some of the things that were presented, and discussed at the convention went against her Catholic upbringing.

She could not, would not, except what she saw or heard.

Elizabeth, on-the-other-hand, was excited and animated, Joseph observed.

"Joseph" she said as she rushed over, grabbed Joseph by the hand, and hustled him over to where she and Christina were sitting.

Elizabeth was fascinated by the Research Society's dedication to the research and documentation of paranormal and occult activities.

One speaker, Dr Goldsten, PH.D, gave a presentation on the Goddess Hecrate, who was, in Greek Mythology, the Patron of Magic, and Witchcraft. Some believers, he said, referred to her as the destroyer and restorer of life. Dr Goldsten went on to say that the Goddess Hecrate believers were known to leave offerings of chicken hearts and cakes to appease her.

Dr Goldsten's presentation sent Elizabeth imagination into overdrive. She wanted to learn and experience more of the mystique surrounding magic and witchcraft.

Elizabeth also grew up under the leadership of the Roman Catholic Church but she never felt fulfilled in her religious studies.

There was something deep inside her that was touched when she listened to people talk on subjects related to the occult.

Sleep came easy for Christina after arriving back at the Hostel; she took a shower and got into bed even though it was only a little after 9pm.

The group had a long and exhausting day; Christina felt its effect both mentally and physically.

Early the next morning she awaken, looked over at the bed next to hers, Elizabeth was not there. Not thinking much of it she rolled over and went back to sleep.

The ringing of the telephone, again, awakens her.

"Hello," she spoke into the receiver.

"Are you guys going down for breakfast?" Joseph asked as Christina attempted to clear her mind. She looked for Elizabeth but did not see her.

"Elizabeth," she called out.

"Elizabeth not here," she told Joseph.

"Were could she be?" he asked.

"Maybe she is downstairs," Christina subjected.

"We had better go and find her," he replied.

Joseph knew of his sister adventures, and some time reckless, behavior. He was angry at her for leaving the room without saying where she was going.

Christina heard the knock on the door. Before she could open it completely Joseph rushed in, he looked at Elizabeth's unmade bed then turned and walked out; Christina followed.

The two went into the Hostel's breakfast bar, no Elizabeth, Joseph ran through the lobby and out onto the streets.

Christina went to the front desk, Philip, the desk clerk; saw the distressed look on her face.

"Is there something wrong," he asked.

"Yes, my cousin didn't sleep in her bed last night; we haven't seen her this morning. Can you check to see if there's a message."

"No miss there's no messages," Philip said, after checking the guest message board.

Joseph was outside pacing in front, he had ran up one side of the street and down the other, looking at the faces of the people pasting, wondering if any one of them has seen Elizabeth.

"Where could she be?" he asked Christina when she joined him on the sidewalk.

"I don't know Joseph, I'm sure she is here somewhere."

III

In the swamps of Plaquemines Parish located in wooded marsh near the Mississippi River, the Grand Bayou Plantation was built in the early part of 1819 by riverboat captains, and pirates.

During its grand days it was a thriving sugar crane plantation with rows of slaves quarter that became the final destination for many African and Haitian slaves.

These slaves bought with them many languages, traditions and religions.

The, predominate, religious belief was that of Ife, which became known as Voudou, today's Voodoo.

After reconstruction, descendants of Haitian slaves purchased the Grand Bayou Plantation, which has remained a spiritual meeting place for Voodouns.

New Orleans have not had a Queen of Voodoo since the death of Marie Laveau in 1881 but her Descendants has remained believers, her teachings has passed from generation to generation.

In 1967, the Grand Bayou Plantation was the site of a Voodoo ritual attended by a young immigrant from a small village called Zooti in southern Togo, West Africa.

**

Binta Adantonwi at age twenty-six boarded a boat, like many others, fleeing the Republic of Togo after the overthrow and killing of then President Olympio in a coup d' etat on January 13, 1963.

On the second night at sea Binta, wet and tired, was awaken by someone tugging at her clothing. She opens her eyes and stared into the face of a man bent over her attempting to remove her dress. She knocks his hand away, rapped her arms around herself as she tried to deny her attacker.

He would not be denied, he hit her with his fist over and over until she relaxed her body and gave in. He removed her dress than exposed himself to her, she closed her eyes when he pushed her legs apart and lay down on top of her.

He thrust himself inside her; she felt pain rush thru her spine up to a spot in her brain that caused something to change in her.

He thrust again and again, she cried out but no help came. When he finished Binta laid weeping, feeling violated.

Over some days Binta and the other women aboard the small boat suffered the same attack from some of the other men aboard.

They were finally rescued by a merchant ship sailing to Port-au-Prince, Haiti.

She and the other African refugees was granted asylum by the government of Haiti. She ended up in the densely populated slums La Saline.

She was not content with this part of Haitian society; she wanted to get to America.

After nearly a year spent in those slums, the opportunity presented itself when she learned of a plan hatched by a group of fishermen to lunch their watercrafts for Florida.

Binta bartered her way onto one of the boats.

Upon entering United States waters many of the boats was turned back by the U.S. Coast Guards, but, a few got through.

Once on the beach of Florida those that made it scattered in different directions, Binta end up at a rest stop frequented by truckers travelling across the country.

She begged for and was granted a ride with a Cajun trucker; Joe LeBlanc.

"Where y'all from?" Joe asked as he shifted gears and merged onto Interstate 10W.

Binta, fluent in French and Portuguese, was not comfortable with English especially not southern slang. She did not really understand Joe's question, it did not matter Joe love to talk, and he was enjoying the companionship. He carried on a conversation with her, even though she barely spoke, all the way to New Orleans.

"Who you know in New Orleans?" Joe questioned Binta.

"Not know," she shook her head when she thought she understood the question.

He did not want to drop her in the middle of New Orleans; he could see that she could use help. He drove her over and left her at the home of Mama Mable.

Mama Mable, who was something of an old Cajun healer, specialized in herbal remedies and Voodoo charms.

People in Plaquemines Parish came to her for all types of ailments to include the removal of hex.

That was more than two years ago, now she moves in tune with to the rhythm of the drums.

She watched as a woman preformed a snake dance that symbolizes the unity between this world and the after life.

The dance is to honor Damballah-Wado, the most supreme Voodoo Loas.

She felt herself losing control, she was being possessed by a spirit, and it was an ancient spirit, a spirit of her ancestor.

The connection to this spirit, she felt, went all the way back to the beginning of her bloodline.

In her mind she believed that she received the message that she will one day be Queen of Ife.

Later that night Binta dreamed that she was presiding over a Voodoo ritual, and been hailed as the Queen.

Some time after she started referring to herself as Lady Binta.

***

Elizabeth, hyped up and full of energy, was too restless to sleep. Not wanting to awaken Christina she went down onto the streets, the humility engulfed her; she immediately began to sweat.

It was late night, the streets had some traffic but it was quiet, the sound of music and voices could be heard in the distance.

Her mind was reflecting on the events of the day as she paced up and down the street in front of the hostel. Sweat ran down her back following the path of her spine.

"What was it Dr Goldsten said?"

"When an evil witch dies, in Cajun belief, ghosts could be sent to attack a victim in their sleep," Elizabeth's mind repeated.

"Could that be true?" she questioned.

A presence could be felt in the dark shadow-less night, no image but there is a presence. A cold chill went thru her causing her teeth to clatter.

A touch, she straighten, looked about, and saw nothing. But the presence was there next to her, all around her.

She could see her breath on the cold still air as she exhaled.

She was engrossed in her own imagination, in her reality she had wondered off the main street and onto one of the many side streets near the hostel.

The bright light of the neon sign snapped her mind out of her daydream.

Lady Binta's Palm Reading & Tarot Cards' the sign read.

Hesitatively Elizabeth approached the store, stopping short of the front door.

A rare breeze blew a warm gust of wind across her face. She noticed the sign, 'Ring for service', hesitating, and overcome by fear, she pushed the button.

Lady Binta, a student of Mama Mable, has experimented with different mixtures and combinations of herbal remedies.

Over the many months of learning from Mama Mable, she has complied; an encyclopedia of pharmaceuticals.

At the time she heard the buzz ringing, she was experimenting with the hallucinogenic properties of wild mushrooms along with tetrodotoxin, a poison found in puffer fish, and datura, a plant known as devil weed.

Tetrodotoxin and Datura when combined can cause a death-like state, and is believed to be use by some vodou practitioner in zombification.

Binta turned the flame off on the pot of boiling herds she was sampling for various teas, and went to answer the buzzer.

"Who dat?" she called out.

"Lady Binta," she heard a voice on the other side of the door call out in return.

"What u want? Child," Binta asked after opening the door just enough to peep out.

The two women glazed into each other eyes and held the stare; a twitch of excitement went thru Elizabeth as she felt drawn to this woman. A feeling of mutual attraction overcame both women.

"Lady Binta?" Elizabeth spoke question-ingly.

"Yes, what u want?" Lady Binta responded.

"A reading," Elizabeth answered while maintaining eye contact.

The cautious expression on Lady Binta's face was quickly replaced by a broad welcoming smile.

She opened the door wide to allow Elizabeth to enter, as Elizabeth passed thru the doorway Binta hesitated expecting others to follow her in.

When no one came thru she peeps outside and saw no one.

***

Nick poured a shot of whiskey into a Styrofoam cup than drunk it down. He dumped the contents of the envelope onto the table.

It contained two investigative reports on a couple of missing Italian females. The reports were prepared by a Detective Robert Forester of the New

Orleans Police Department, who had been assigned to investigate the disappearances.

Detective Forester reports that a Joseph Randazo, a visitor from Rome, Italy, filed a missing person report on a Elizabeth Randazo, his sister, on 18 August 1969 at 1048am.

The report contains a statement obtained from Christina Randazo, a cousin of the missing person, from Levanzo, Italy.

Also included was a statement from the staff of the New Orleans International Hostel on Carondelet Street.

Detective Forester noted interviewing a Susan Johnson, a committee member of the New Orleans Paranormal and Occult Research Society. Ms Johnson, as Detective Forester wrote, confirms that Elizabeth and Christina attended their convention at the Ramada Hotel.

Nick took special note of this interview, he wondered why had the two women attended. There was nothing in the report that pointed to foul play or what may have happened to Elizabeth Randazo.

He pushed back from the table and folded his hands together behind his head and stared out the dirty window of this cheap hotel.

He figured that he would ask the three Frank's to setup a meeting with Detective Forester so he could probe the detective for information not in his report.

The sounds from the next room was quieter, the sounds of wild sex was replaced by heavy snoring.

Nick lay down on the bed, fully clothed, and was asleep soon after.

***

Lady Binta sits listening to Elizabeth talk about her life in Rome. She truly believes that her destiny is to be Queen of Voodoo in New Orleans, since receiving what she interpreted as a message from her ancestors.

She has been preparing herself by studying the history, the underlining traditions of ceremonies, and practices as they were preformed by Voodouns in this city.

She has been seen in the company of a powerful Hoodoo witchdoctor, Julien Sinclare.

Rumor has it that Binta is one of Sinclare's three wives. She used her association with Sinclare to absorb as much as she could of his knowledge of psychological manipulation, which he was an expert.

Elizabeth volunteered a lot of information about herself and her relationship with her father, which was usually strained.

"I have always been fascinated with the unknown," Elizabeth offered.

"There are forces operating beyond human understanding, what is it that you want to know?" Lady Binta asked Elizabeth, as her mind reflected on what force was in play that had brought this woman to seek her out.

"Can you tell me something about the future?" Elizabeth asked.

Lady Binta stared at Elizabeth; she was silently asking Damballah-Wedo for clarity.

She was becoming convinced that Elizabeth showing up alone, seeking guidance, was not by chance.

The two women eyes locked, a tingle of electricity caused Elizabeth's heart to beat faster.

She looked away, embarrassed and confessed by her feelings of attraction.

Lady Binta took note of Elizabeth's reaction, she felt drawn to the young woman. She decided that she would recruit Elizabeth as her first disciple.

"Let's see how the card reads," Lady Binta said, in response to Elizabeth's question.

She got up from the table, walked over, opened the drawer to the desk in what was used as a reception area.

Binta took out a deck of Major Arcana tarot cards and placed them on the table.

She left the room, entered the kitchen where she filled a tea kittle with water and placed it on low flames.

She returned and took her seat at the table across from Elizabeth.

She gave a silent prayer to the gods before picking up the cards and shuffled.

"Are you opened to what the cards have to say?" she asked.

Elizabeth thought about the question, and then asked "Why did you ask me this?"

"The cards are mysterious they don't always give the answers we want. You have to trust in the answer given," Lady Binta explained.

The question was asked in order to probe Elizabeth's accessibility to suggestions; Elizabeth's response gave Binta the answer.

The first card Lady Binta flipped over was 'Strength'; she explained that this card stresses discipline and control. The lion represents the primal part of the mind and the woman, the higher or elevated parts of the mind. Inner-strength that is used in fighting an internal battle.

The next card was 'The Moon' which Binta explains to represents life of the imagination. The dog and wolf are fears of the natural mind and the moon is the reflection of intellectual light and beyond it is the unknown mystery which it cannot reveal.

Lady Binta hesitated, drawing out the suspense, as the hissing sound of the tea kittle disturbed the silence.

She sits up straight in her chair, and gave a sigh of disbelief. She looked at Elizabeth with skeptical eyes. But, the cards had confirmed her perception that the spirits had sent Elizabeth to her.

When the final card was revealed, 'The High Priestess',

Lady Binta interpreted this as been otherworldliness or a mystical vision, not Elizabeth's but hers.

"What does it say about my future?" Elizabeth questioned.

Binta did not answer immediately, her mind was racing, and she had to keep Elizabeth from leaving and under her control.

"Tea," she finally said.

"What?" Elizabeth responded.

"I will make us a cup of tea, then we will talk of the future," Lady Binta explained.

As Elizabeth sipped the tea, Lady Binta began telling the story of her childhood in the village of Zooti in West Africa.

"When I was a child my parents told me the stories pasted down from the ancestors. They would tell how the practice of our religion has changed. We, like our ancestors, believe in Ife and we worship spirits. But unlike the way things are done today the ancestors honored the spirits with human sacrifices to appease them," Binta paused.

Elizabeth was intrigued with the story and asked, "You said that you belief in Ife. What is it?"

Lady Binta smiled to herself, Elizabeth had taken the bait, and all she had to do was to excite her imagination.

"You might know it by the name that it is referred today, Voodoo."

Tic, tic, Elizabeth looked over to where the clock hung on the wall, *tic, tic, tic,* the sound of the clock echoed in her ear.

She squinted as she looked at the lamp on the table.

The dimly illuminated bulb seems to have brightened, as the hallucinogenic herbs in the tea took effect, causing heightened senses.

Binta noticed the glaze in Elizabeth's eyes knew the drugs had started to work.

"What did you put in the tea?" Elizabeth demanded as her mind drifted farther away from her control.

"Drum beats," Elizabeth's mind registered.

The rhythmic beat of the drum from a recording of a Voodoo ritual was playing in the background.

Lady Binta started playing the recording when Elizabeth's attention was on the flicker of flame, from the candle on a stand that held a picture of Binta dressed in a white headdress and white gown.

The drum beat in the background caused Elizabeth's body to move in tune with the rhythm.

She got up from the table, started to dance slowly with the beat.

A flood of sexual stimulus flowed, as her movement became more erotic with the change in tempo of the beat.

Coupled with the chanting of the crowd; Elizabeth was hot, not only from the humility but also, from the stimulation of the drug.

She was slowly been possessed by the chants and calls of the people on the recording.

She started removing articles of clothing one at a time until she was fully naked.

Still dancing to be beat, she felt a presence hovering over her.

Elizabeth was now on her hands and knees thrusting her pelvis backward and forward. A soft mumble came from her lips as she took up the chant of the people.

All the while Lady Binta stood next to Elizabeth chanting and instructing, planting the seeds of control.

Elizabeth's eyes flew opened as though startle, she was lying in a bed naked, and intertwined with the naked body of Lady Binta.

Binta's head rested on her hands with her elbow propped on a pillow. She looked down on Elizabeth whose eyes, filled with confession, tried to focus on her.

Elizabeth tried to setup but was overcome by nausea, she laid back down.

"How did I get here?" Elizabeth finally asked.

"Don't you remember our little party?" Lady Binta interjected.

Elizabeth concentrated hard, trying to blow away the cloud that blanketed her brain. Slowly she started to recall.

Her body began to respond to Lady Binta's touch as the memory of the buildup to, and the release of, ecstasy came back.

She jumped up and out of bed.

"You drugged me. Where are my clothes?" she demanded.

"There on the chair. But you cannot leave."

"What are you saying? I must go; my brother will be looking for me."

"He will not find you," Lady Binta's tone was getting more threatening.

Elizabeth felt trapped, but she was intrigued, than easily accepted the facts of the situation that she was in.

The door to the bedroom swing open, Elizabeth's heart skipped a beat; she took a few steps backward when Sinclare entered the room.

Elizabeth's reaction gave Sinclare a since of pleasure and accomplishment, he relished in his ability to enliven fear in others.

He was the darkest and biggest man Elizabeth had encountered.

Sinclare stood in the doorway shirtless with bulging muscles. Even in his later years, he was intimidating.

Elizabeth could barely make out the tattoo's covering his dark skin.

Lady Binta grunted and shooed him away. Sinclare gave a deep baritone round of laughter as he backed out of the room.

"Who was that?" Elizabeth asked, still frightened.

"Some old witchdoctor," was Lady Binta's answer.

"Witchdoctor," Elizabeth turned, stared at Binta, hoping for more information. "Why did you bring me here?"

"It was in the cards" Lady Binta proclaimed.

"The cards? Where am I?" Elizabeth demanded.

***

"Mother of God" Christina started her prayer, as she knelt facing the cross at the Church of Saint Mary of Jesus.

She has prayed everyday since arriving back in Levanzo.

Christina and Joseph spent an additional three months in America after reporting Elizabeth missing, nearly a year ago.

Christina was happy to be home and in the care of her parents. She had enough of Joseph's belittling and hurtful remarks.

"You selfish little brat, how could you just let her go off alone?" he would say.

Joseph took Elizabeth's disappearance hard, he was angry and feeling helpless.

After the first week Joseph started drinking heavily and became a noisome for the New Orleans Police Department.

During the day he spent most of his time on the phone, calling the NOPD or, talking with his father.

Antonio Randazo put his son in contact with the Italian Honorary Consulate on North Causeway in New Orleans. He expected to receive regular updates.

Joseph drowned his feeling of guilt with scotch-on-the-rocks in the hostel's lounge.

When alcohol didn't work at controlling his self-degradation, he sought out Christina to ridicule.

Christina, holding tight to her faith, prayed that Elizabeth would return. She also prayed for Joseph to get strong enough to overcome his demons.

Saint Joseph's Catholic Church became her sanctuary.

At night Joseph could be found at the Howln' Wolf. He had developed a reputation as a decent horn player and a heavy scotch drinker.

It was under the threat of arrest and urging from the consulate that Joseph agreed to return to Rome.

Christina was seating in silent's when Father Paul came and sit next to her.

The quietness of the church sanctuary provided the atmosphere for refection. Father Paul's presence aided Christina's feeling of connection, at that moment, to the omnipresence of God.

"I have prayed for Elizabeth everyday. But I have doubts," Christina said, breaking the silence.

"Elizabeth has always been unpredictable. When we were together in America she insisted that we attend a conference on paranormal and the occult. Afterward Elizabeth was restless, she became distant. And there's this," Christina handed Father Paul the poster of the sabbatical goat that Elizabeth had purchased.

"Elizabeth has had a fascination," Christina continued, "with the supernatural and other secular beliefs for as long as I can remember."

"I'm sure that it's nothing to worry yourself over. We all know of Elizabeth's quizzical personality," Father Paul said.

Christina allowed Father Paul's comment to past without much thought. She was trying to work out her own emotional conflicts.

"Father what can you tell me about that?" Christina asked, pointing to the poster.

Father Paul hesitated, than stared into the eyes of the image represented on the poster. Been a student of religious history, he knew something about the time period.

"It is my understanding that the image first appeared in the 19th century as a figure for Satanism. It was a representation of Baphomet which was a pagan deity. There have been many books written about Baphomet. It may be good for you to do your own research," Father Paul encouraged.

"Father I don't think that Elizabeth would just go off without saying something. I believe that she walked into a situation beyond her control. But I do doubt the search for her will led to finding her," Christina said.

"Why the doubts?" Father Paul asked.

"Elizabeth's imagination went into overdrive after Dr Goldstein's presentation. She wanted to learn more about the mystique surrounding magic and witchcraft," Christina explained.

"I don't thank that Elizabeth wants to be found," she concluded.

***

Elizabeth's father had gotten frustrated with what he considered incompetence on the behalf of the New Orleans Police Department.

The dwindling support from the Italian Embassy farther lent itself to his feeling of isolation.

Motivated by his fears for his wife's stated of mind, Antonio Randazo, decided to travel to America and the city of New Orleans.

He discussed his plans with Christina's father, who agreed that Christina should take the trip with her uncle if she would agree.

IV

Nick's wounds took months to heal after he, and, a number of, other French soldiers' was ambushed by rebels in Chad.

He was setting in his office reflecting on his last mission with the Legion. His memories were trigged by a news article: "Eleven French Soldiers killed in a shootout with rebels in Chad."

Nick absentmindedly rubbed his wounds as he read the news. "Sir," his office assistant disturbed his rememorizing.

"This just arrived," she said handing him the letter.

The letter was addressed to Cleo Nickelson Detective Agency, Naples. The name of the sender brought a smile; he thanked his assistant then sits back in his chair and opened the letter.

Antonio Palermo, son of Frank Palermo head of the Palermo mafia in Levanzo; did a short tour with the French Foreign Legion.

Nick and Antonio served together in Northern Africa. The two became battle buddies, close associates, after Antonio's tour he, and Nick did not remain in contact.

The letter was a welcome surprise.

Nick arrived early for his meeting with Antonio at the Rose Garden Palace in Rome. Antonio's letter contained a telephone number and a request for Nick to call immediately. After speaking briefly over the phone the men agreed to meet.

Nick sits at a table near the rear of the restaurant with his back to the wall so that he would have a clear vision of who was entering and leaving.

The Rose Garden Palace was a small intimate restaurant with traditional Italian décor. Nick ordered coffee, glanced over the menu, and waited.

He saw Antonio enter the restaurant accompanied by a mid-aged attractive female. She was casually dressed in a white opened blouse tugged into a black skirt that complimented her figure.

Reading her body language as she made her way thru the restaurant, Nick concluded that this was a difficult prudish woman.

"Cleo," Antonio shouted as he approached, extending his hand. Antonio was one of a handful of people that called Nick by his first name.

"Antonio," Nick responded as he stood and extended his hand. The men shook hands in greeting.

"Cleo I would like to introduce you to my wife, and the love of my life," Antonio said as he placed his arm around the woman standing next to him.

"Cleo this is Carmella; Carmella this is my old friend Cleo Nickelson," Antonio made the introduction.

It was Carmella plea, and Nick's desire to help an old friend, are the reasons why he finds himself about to meet with Detective Forester of the New Orleans Police Department.

He was under no illusion; his tasks will be difficult ones. He was hired to achieve something that the NOPD have yet to accomplish.

Antonio and Carmella hired Nick to locate, or uncover information about, the two missing Italian women. Carmella explained that the Randazo family was grieving over the disappearance of two member of the family. Both occurring in New Orleans, nearly two years apart.

Detective Forester was setting at the bar, socializing with the bartender and one of the Frank's,

when Nick entered Razzo Bar & Bistro. He walked up to the bar and ordered a scotch-n-water. After a brief introduction Frank left the men to their business, Nick and Detective Forester took seats at a table.

"We still don't have a lot of information on

the first missing young lady, Elizabeth," Detective Forester began discussing the case.

"She seems to have just vanished after leaving the International Hostel. We have turned up no witnesses."

"I believe that I will concentrate on the last young woman that went missing, Christina Randazo. What do you have on her case?" Nick asked.

"What we know," Detective Forester began a narration of his investigation. "Christina and her uncle, Antonio Randazo, arrived in New Orleans about four months ago."

The lunch crowd was arriving at Razzo's; the restaurant was filling up fast. The smell of garlic, pasta, and baked bread made Nick's mouth water, and his stomach growl. He was pleased when a waiter placed bread and spread on the table, and then asked for their orders.

Detective Forester continued his brief summary after placing an order for, Linguine with cuttlefish and ink sauce with steamed sea bass.

"As you may know, Antonio Randazo is the father of Elizabeth Randazo the first missing woman. Christina Randazo alone with Joseph Randazo, the bother of Elizabeth, was here when Elizabeth disappeared. It was Joseph that reported her missing."

"Yes, I read all that in your report. What I like is something that's not in the report. What is your gut telling you what happened to Christina?" Nick pressed.

Nick noticed that the three Franks had appeared in the restaurant and was chatting, and socializing with the crowd. It seemed out of character to him because he knew that these guys was deadly mobsters.

"The telephone call that Christina received, which, I believe, was the motivation that prompted her to leave the Hostel. Possibly came from someone with knowledge of Elizabeth's whereabouts.

Maybe even from Elizabeth herself. Either way I think that Elizabeth is alive somewhere in the city. One of the unanswered questions is who knew that Christina and her uncle was here looking for information about Elizabeth?" Detective Forester surmised.

***

The heavy rains that blanketed New Orleans during the day had slowly moved to the east, along with the dark clouds, and 20mph winds.

The ground was water soaked, the night air cool, and a light fog was moving over the city.

Plaquemines Parish was eerily quite a hazy glow could be seen through the fog for some distances. The crowd of people that had gathered mulled around in anticipation, warmed by the heat from the bonfire.

Beyond the light of the fire, it was pitched dark the sounds of crickets chirping in the swamp could be heard over the wispier voices.

The beat of the drums signaled that the rituals were about to began.

Among the Voodouns of Plaquemines Parish Julien Sinclare is a powerful Nanga who is believed to be an intermediary between human and the spirits.

Sinclare's legend has grown over the years; he is widely respected for his holistic healing powers.

For a week word had past, thru the Parishes, that a special healing ritual would be preformed tonight. Word has it that Sinclare would be guiding a lost soul back into the arms of the ancestors.

The rhythm beats vibrating through the crowd took control of the believers causing them to dance to the sound of the drums. As the people danced a call to the ancestors begun to be chanted.

The glow from the fire's flame cast long shadows that added drama to the scene.

As the beat of the drums slowed a hush fall over the crowd; Binta appeared among the people dressed in traditional white garb carrying a white python high over her head.

Sinclare followed Binta, dressed in full Zimbabwean witch doctor garb, towards the bonfire carrying the limp body of Elizabeth; he placed her on the wet earth near the fire.

Binta started the snake dance to the serpent god, Damballah-Wedo, symbolizing unity with the spirit world. Binta and the python danced as though one with the ancestors.

Elizabeth laid motionless on the ground not able the move, her mind was fully aware of all the activity surrounding her. She could feel the wet earth beneath her, and the warmth of the bonfire.

She could hear the beat of the drums, and the chants of the people, she also saw Binta dancing with the snake. The one thing she was not able to do was move her body, she had no control.

Sinclare had prepared a special tea for Elizabeth to drank, one that put her body in a temporary zombie state. He was a master performer.

Sinclare sat cross-legged, eyes closed in meditation, on the ground next to Elizabeth while Binta continued dancing to the serpent god.

As the drug started to wear off, Elizabeth body began to move in groove with the beat, Sinclare appeared in her head beckoning her to come to him.

As the spirits of the ancestors took control of people in the crowd, Elizabeth appeared to have floated upright onto her feet.

She was in a trance, a spirit of her ancestor, from her people's bloodline, was controlling her movement. She was mimicking Binta's snake dance.

Elizabeth was possessed, and all the while Sinclare was there with her; in her head.

Sinclare was on his feet high stepping circling the two women and the python. The crowd was in a frantic, the beats from the drums came faster; the whole scene was out of control.

For hours the people danced in honor of the serpent god Damballah-Wedo.

Elizabeth felled to her knees, exhausted, at some point in the dance she took control of the python which was now rapped around her.

One-by-one the people felled from exhaustion, the beat of the drums slowed as the ancestor's spirits took their leave.

Sinclare stayed behind to heal the sick while Binta led Elizabeth away; to the main house on the plantation.

Elizabeth was now counted among the believers.

.

Elizabeth continued, months later, to be under the watchful eyes of Binta, and those that lived at the plantation.

She was not allowed to leave, but she had freedom of movement on the grounds of the plantation, she was also learning.

Binta was expanding her range of influence among New Orleans Voodoo practitioners, she has recruited a number of followers, but she still considered Elizabeth her prize convert. She was spending more and more time fellowshipping with the people of Plaquemines Parish.

Elizabeth was left in the care of the other two women at the plantation. She was feeling more isolated, when Binta was there she at less had someone to talk with.

Binta was also teaching her herbal medicine, and ways to combat evil spirits.

Elizabeth started to experiment on her own; she improvised; used different combination of herbs. She had gotten to a point were her expanding knowledge went beyond Binta's teachings.

Late in the evening when the two women was not paying her much attention. Elizabeth would slip out of the house and sneak down, where in years past would have been the slave quarters, to watch Sinclare perfect his conjuring and other magic.

Elizabeth began to develop her own plan as to how she would escape the restrictions of the plantation.

It was obvious for Elizabeth to see that Binta was the dominate female here, but Sinclare was the shot caller.

People from all over sought his counsel for all types to problems, or they would ask for his blessing.

She decided that the best way for her to escape her confinement was to gain favor with Sinclare.

What Elizabeth hadn't realized was that Sinclare was aware of her presence when, she thought that he did not know she was spying on him when he was consulting with the ancestors.

Sinclare is a shrewd operator, he was not often fooled by others intentions. He would allow Elizabeth to pursue her foolish plan because he was pursuing a plan of his own.

Nick's move into the New Orleans International Hostel made it easier for him to pursue some of the information that Detective Forester provided; starting with who did Christina and her uncle speak to.

The desk clerk that received the phone call, and transferred it to Christina's room, was the first person that Nick interviewed.

He knew from the police report that the call was made from a pay phone near the intersection of River Road and Bridge City Avenue; that the voice on the phone was that of a woman.

Days before, Antonio Randazo was seen showing Elizabeth's photograph to the staff of the hostel and to some of the businesses in the neighborhood.

The cab driver drove across the Huey P. Long Bridge, traveling the same route which he had driven Christina. The cab dropped Nick off at Café Armanda, the same spot he had taken Christina.

The manager of Café Armanda is a Haitian immigrant, Delon Pierre.

Mr. Pierre, since immigrating, converted, from practicing Voodoo, to Catholicism. He still has connections to the Voodoun's community through friends and family who kelp him abreast of what was happening within the community.

The rumors and reputation of Lady Binta has been circulated throughout the whole of New Orleans Voodoo society.

There was some that revered her, and some that feared her rumored use of evil spirits to hex those that apposed her.

It had been note in Detective Forester's report that Mr. Pierre had been interviewed, and that he had provided information that confirmed that Christina was at the Café Armanda on the day she went missing, and that she had been approached by, and had a conversation with a known hustler that goes by the handle, 'Silky'.

"Thanks for meeting with me," Nick said, as he introduced himself to Delon Pierre.

"Don't mention it. Detective Forester said that the family of the missing young woman sent you to help," Delon said.

"Yes, the family is very worried; at the same time is willing to do everything to find Christina," Nick.

"Like I've told Detective Forester, she was here sitting over there at that table that faces out onto the street. She was here about twenty minutes when this guy, 'Silky', came in, and struck up a conversation with her that lasted approximately fifteen to twenty minutes. She was still sitting there when he left," Delon explained.

"What can you tell me about this Silky?" Nick asked.

"I only know the reputation, not the man. He is said to be an Alabama fellow that came to New Orleans a few years ago. He is a low level pimp that operates in the Quarters. I have seen him in here from time to time looking for young vulnerable ladies," Delon summarized.

"How long did she stay here after he left?" Nick asked.

"For a good half-hour."

"Have Silky been around since that day?" Nick.

"No, haven't seen him."

"I'll like to thank you again for your time. I'm staying at the New Orleans International Hostel over on Carondelet Street, just in case," Nick.

Nick walked out of Café Armanda, onto River Road, took a deep breath; he felt that he had a good start. He notice the taxis stand a few block up River Road and headed in that direction.

He showed the photographs of the two missing women to a few of the drivers mulling around the stand and got a curious responds from one.

The driver, a Cajun, looked at both pictures but focused his attention on Elizabeth's.

Shaking his head while handing the photos back to Nick, he said, "High Priestess."

Nick hired the cabby to drive him to Razzo's on Bourbon Street.

"What did you mean when you referred to this photo as High Priestess?" Nick asked the driver as he held up Elizabeth's photograph.

"Didn't mean anything," was the only thing the driver would say.

The three Frank's was seating at the table in their office, again they were eating what looked like a full course meal. They each looked up and greeted Nick when he walked thru the door.

"Have a seat, Mr. PI", one of the Frank's said to Nick.

"How's it going?" another one asked.

"Can we get you something to drink," the same one offered.

"Yes; scotch-n-water. I need help locating a guy," Nick responded.

"Who is this guy?"

"A locate guy, I was told that he is a pimp/ hustler that operates in the Quarters that goes by the name, Silky," Nick.

"No problem," the three Frank's spoke, in unison.

A few days later Nick was in his room at the International Hostel when he received a message from the Frank's, "the guy haven't been seen around in weeks, keep you informed."

V

The women, of Grand Bayou Plantation, were gathered around the dining table made of solid oak, listening to a recording of a Swazi Sangoma praying-chant.

Binta had received the recording, that day, from one of the oldest surviving descendant of one of the freed slaves that had purchased the plantation after reconstruction, today the name on the title to the property is that of Julien Sinclare.

An elderly female spoke the voice, scratchy and wearisome, in heavy accented English.

Elizabeth listened intensely, she internalized and indentified with the words spoken, when the speaker prayed to the ancestral spirits for relief from damnation and be provided a place in the after life.

The other three woman took note of Elizabeth, her eyes were closed, as she listened, she was swaying with the pitches in the voice on the recording.

Binta felt like a proud parent as she watched Elizabeth.

Out of the darkness, in Elizabeth's mind, Sinclare appeared in a glow of light with his arms outstretched, Elizabeth tried to go towards him, but his image faded farther and farther into the distance, and than disappeared.

Early the next morning, before the crest of day, Elizabeth slipped out of the house and down to the cabin were Sinclare was sitting cross legged by a low fire, meditating.

She quietly positioned herself, in the darkness, and watched. A light fog had settled over the swamp, the air was cool, and smell of smoke from the fire dominated.

Sinclare stood up and started moving around; Elizabeth lost sight of him; moved from her position to see what he was doing. She froze, daring not to turnaround, she knew, because she could feel his presence that Sinclare was behind her.

Slowly she turned and looked up into his eyes, he stared down into her; she felt, not fear, a sense of out-of-body sensation, he was controlling her thoughts.

He towered over her, his musk attacked her senses making her slightly dizzy, beside for the tattoos, and body paint, Sinclare was naked.

Elizabeth's eyes moved from Sinclare's down to his loin, where his member dangled, touching her. He turned and walked back towards the cabin, she followed.

Inside the small one room cabin Elizabeth was engulfed by a layer of smoke from a combination of burning incenses, and sage plants.

There was no bed, a mattress laid on the floor covered by a hand sewed quilt. She undid the buttons that held her dress, allowed it to fall to the floor.

She laid down onto the makeshift bed and offered herself to Sinclare; she had no will nor desires to stop herself.

He stood, looking down on her, as she reached for his member and began to stroke; the weight of it in her hand caused her to get excited with anticipation.

Sinclare knelt down, slowly rubbed her stomach at the bellybutton, he moved his hand, slowly, up to caress her breasts.

She opened, pushed her chest forward offering them to him. His fingers, slowly, made their way to her lips; she opened her mouth and ran her tongue around the tips.

His hand slid down her body, came to rest between her legs; Elizabeth pushed herself up to her knees, threw her arms around his neck, and pulled Sinclare down on top of her.

She reached for his member, guided it into her moist opening, her womb enclosed on him as he slid inside. She had to bit her lip to suppress the pain, when he pushed deeper inside.

Pain turned into pleasure as she thrust upward to meet his downward thrust.

Tingles of pleasure cascaded thru her, she lost herself in the act, moaning and thrusting wildly, again and again she thrust, each time more violently, trying to engulf all of him.

He pushed deeper than before, the scream came from a place buried in a hidden place of her soul, echoing in her ears, as her essence released the same time he exploded inside her.

She went limp, shaking under him, rapping her legs around him, she held on tight burying her head into his shoulder, she sobbed.

He rolled off, she jumped up, pick up her dress, and ran back to the main house, struggling with feelings of confusion, and gratification.

Binta sensed a change in Elizabeth, started to watch her with more vigilance, she couldn't figure out what had caused the change. "She must be under some spell," Binta thought to herself.

Elizabeth, feeling more mature and less timed, started to challenge Binta's influence; re-buffed her unreasonable demands.

Binta has spent years developing her skills, and positioning herself, so she could be recognized as Queen of New Orleans Voodoo. The ideal that Elizabeth was not shown her the respect nor revenants she thought she desired sent Binta into rages that bordered on madness.

Elizabeth felt that she no longer needed to sneak down to watch Sinclare at his cabin; she would boldly go down and sit cross-legged with Sinclare as he meditated.

Inside the cabin, along one wall, a long narrow table held what only could only be described as a chemical lab where an assortment of plants, herbs, and equipment including tests tubes, and a microscope was displayed.

Elizabeth would watch as Sinclare test different plants, and extract its chemical compound for use in healing or for making poisons.

The fearsome image of the man she first laid eyes was less so today.

Elizabeth's admiration for Sinclare grew each time she discovered something new about him.

She took it upon herself to be his caretaker,

preparing food and insuring that his herb tea, which he drinks each morning, was exactly as he like it.

This donning of affection, and attention, paid to Sinclare's needs farther angered Binta, who was openly showing sign of frustration with Elizabeth's behavior.

Legions between the four women began to form into two camps, with Binta and Elizabeth opposing one another.

***

Detective Forester telephoned the International Hostel at 0500am on August 15, 1974, asked to be connected to Nick's room.

"I understand that you have been looking for a guy," the Detective said when hearing Nick's voice in the receiver.

"Yes, do you have a lead on him?" Nick asked.

"Get dressed, I will pick you up in a half-hour," Detective Forester commanded.

They arrived at Bayou St John, crossed over the yellow crime scene tape.

The led homicide Detective, Dennis McCoy, greeted Detective Forester with a, 'good old buddy', handshake.

"Is this the PI from Rome?" Detective McCoy asked.

"Yes, this is Cleo Nickerson," Detective Forester introduced Nick

.

Nick stuck out his hand, expecting a returned handshake but did not receive one.

Detective McCoy just gave Nick an investigative look over and turned away.

"What do you have Mac?" Detective Forester asked.

"I believe this is your guy, Leroy Anderson, aka Silky," Detective McCoy said, as he removed the white sheet covering the dead body.

"What happened here Mac?" Detective Forester asked.

Nick and Detective Forester followed Detective McCoy, about fifty yards away from where the body laid, to where the remnants of a bonfire, and blood splatters were visible on the ground, and on a makeshift altar.

"Looks like there was Voodoo activity here. Your dead guy?" Detective McCoy pointed to where Silky's stiff body laid. "Looks like poison. According to Forensic he has been here about three days," Detective McCoy explained how his investigation was proceeding.

"You think this has something to do with the missing woman?" Nick asked."

"Possibly, or it could be just coincidence that the guy that approached Christina at the restaurant ended up dead. And looking at the location, which is a possible site used by people that practice Voodoo," Detective Forester interjected.

"Are there many people that practice Voodoo in New Orleans?" Nick.

"Yes, its part of the culture in some quarters," Detective McCoy explained.

"How do you know that the site was used for Voodoo?" Nick.

"Well we don't know for sure yet, it could have been staged to look that way to throw us off. Some of the signs that points in that direction of Voodoo is the blood splattered, human or animal we do not know yet, says that a sacrifice was offered. The remnants of what looks like a bonfire, and over here", the two men followed Detective McCoy to a large pine tree where he pointed to an object nailed to the tree, "looks like someone has been threaten with evil spirits", Detective McCoy summarized.

Back in his room, Nick had a lot to maul over; he decided to learn more about the Voodoo culture in New Orleans.

In his native country, Kabylie, Algeria, spirit worshiping is part of the fabric of the land itself. He did not know how the religion was practiced outside of Algeria.

He remembered, from Detective Forester's report, that Elizabeth and Christina had attended a convention held by the New Orleans Paranormal and Occult Research Society and decided to contact them to gain more of an insight into the people who practice Voodoo in Louisiana.

***

Susan Johnson, who holds a masters degree in religious studies, wrote her college thesis on the religious practices of the indigenous, Norte Chico, people of South America, is a member of a five person committee that studies witchcraft, and ghost phenomenon, met with Nick at the Research Society's office on Fontainebleau Drive.

"You said on the phone that you were investigating the disappearance of two women," Ms Johnson questioned.

"Yes, the women were both Italian citizens and members of the same family. They were here visiting when they disappeared, strangely it was ap-

proximately two years between disappearances",
Nick answered.

"And you think that Voodoo had something
to do with the missing women?" Susan.

"I can't say at this point, I am just following
a few leads. Any information you can provide
would be helpful."

Susan Johnson explained that in Voodoo,
like most religions, including Catholicism, the levels
of devotion varies from person-to-person. And, the
effect upon the devotee depends on the strength of
ones beliefs.

"Voodoo core beliefs include the recognition
of one God who avoids interfering in the daily lives
of people, and spirits that preside over the daily
lives of its followers.

Kind and mischievous spiritual forces shape
the lives of Voudoun's from the beginning up to today. The connection with these spirits can be
achieved through dance, music, singing, and the use

of snakes, which is the main spiritual conduit to all others.

Deceased ancestors can also intercede in the lives of Voodoo followers," Susan narrated, and she added, "Voodoo was brought to the French colony of Louisiana by slaves starting in 1719."

""How widespread is the practice here? Are there prominent members of the Voodoo community?" Nick wanted to know.

"Yes, witchdoctors, and other healers with knowledge of herbs, charms and amulets preparation, and poisons, are held in high esteem. There is one name that seems to carry more weight within the community, Julien Sinclare," Susan acknowledged.

"One last thing, what message is been sent by nailing a Voodoo doll covered by a chickens foot to a tree?"

"Where did you see this?"

"A dead body was found at Bayou St John's, a few yards away the police discovered it," Nick explained.

"Voodoo dolls are rarely used in curses; they are usually used in blessings and are forms of gris-gris that is made for people seeking love; power; luck that sort of thing. In this instance it could be simply a warning," Susan offered.

VI

The weather in New Orleans had turned, for most of the week the skies where clear with mild sunny days, heavy rain rolled across the city bring flashes of lighten followed by rolling thunder that vibrated far into the distance.

Puddles of water accumulated in the street outside of Binta's Palm Reading Parlor, the wind could be heard whistling past the window.

"He think that he can use sorcery to steal her," Binta was talking to herself as she mixed jimson weed and sulphur into hot water to form a tea.

She poured the mixture into a cup, added honey, than took the cup over to where she had a black cat tided by a string, and rubbed the cup against the cat, than Binta slowly sipped the mixture.

This recipe she was sure would war off any spell that had affected Elizabeth.

She prayed for guidance from the most powerful of loas, Iwa Damballah Welo, before laying the doll, made from pieces of Elizabeth's clothing, stuffed with leaves from an imphepho plant, and sewn together with strings of Elizabeth's hair, on the table.

She placed the photograph of Elizabeth over the doll, and began her chant.

At the same instant, Thomas knocked on the door to the house of Grand Bayou Plantation, he fail to the floor, convulsing, when Elizabeth answered his knocks.

She stepped back in horror; momentarily shocked at the sight of him. A calmness came over her as the healer inside sprung into action, she helped Thomas up, took him to the den, laid him on the floor.

"Hexed," he whisper in her ear.

She left him lying on the floor and went into the kitchen, put water in a tea kittle, placed it on high flames. Holding a towel under cool water she thought about the ingredients.

With the wet towel she returned to Thomas, and placed it on his head then knelt down, started to chant the same Swazi Sangoma praying-chant she had heard on the recording in his ear.

The effect was immediate, his heart rate stabilized, a warmth came over him that eased his chills.

She left his side, when back into the kitchen, she put datura, jimson weed, sulphur, and honey into a cup, poured in hot water to make a cure-all tea.

She helped Thomas prop himself up against the wall, as he sipped the tea she chanted the Swazi Sangoma praying-chant while passing the tail of a black cat over him from head to toe.

It didn't take long before Thomas started to respond positively to the herbs.

With his fever broken he stared at Elizabeth in confused curiosity, so thankful to be relieved of his torment he bent over, kissed her feet in a sign of loyalty than jumped up and dashed out the front door.

Antonio Randazo was up early, he wanted to get an early start passing out Elizabeth's photograph and speak with as many people he could before his appointment at the Italian Consulate.

He posted the Elizabeth's photo on several businesses, with the telephone number to the International Hostel, and his name, in the area surrounding the hostel.

Binta was convinced that the gris-gris would break the spell Sinclare had on Elizabeth; she was leaving her studio when she noticed the photograph taped to the window.

She took the photo, went back inside and called the telephone number, the desk clerk at the International Hostel answered, she asked to be connected to the room of Mr. Randazo; no one answered.

She hung-up and made another phone call. Silky, who has become a strong believer in Binta's powers as a healer, and intermediary to the spirits, arrived a little over an hour after Binta's call.

Together they hatched a plan that would allow Silky to find out who was putting up Elizabeth's photograph, and what information they were seeking.

He was to hang around the International Hostel, gather what information he could, and report back to Binta.

Whispers of Elizabeth spread throughout Plaquemines Parish from person-to-person after Thomas, who couldn't contain his gratitude, started to tell how she saved him from evil magic.

People started to wonder about this unknown stranger who possessed such powers. Rumors, backed by other rumors, made her out to be the product of Sinclare's conjuring.

"I don't know where she came from."

"I went out to Grand Bayou's looking for help from Lady Binta and she answered the door, I was in bad shape, she cured me. It was like she was some high priestess or something," Thomas would tell people.

Word of Thomas's story got to Binta, who first doubted the story, from people; she trusted whose loyalty was unquestioning.

She began to see the story as another challenge to her destiny, especially because it reportedly happened at the plantation.

She put word out that Thomas was a disloyal liar who has dishonored the ancestors. This proclamation put Thomas's life, she knew, in danger.

When word that Lady Binta had claimed him dishonorable got back to Thomas, he was so fearful that he committed suicide by jumping to his death from the Huey P. Long Bridge.

"I do not fear you," Elizabeth shouted.

She and Binta were face-to-face in the middle of Sinclare's, who had left the plantation, cabin.

"You stupid little girl, can't you see that he has used magic on you?" Binta questioned.

"What I know is that it was you who drugged me, brought me here, and kelp me against my will," Elizabeth responded.

"Against your will? Ha! You could have left this place along time ago. You have had the freedom to roam freely, you could have walk away anytime," Binta reminded Elizabeth. "Sinclare," she continued "has put a spell on you. How else can you explain your behavior; seeing to his every need?"

Elizabeth knew that Binta spoke the truth; she hadn't attempted to leave not even the first day she arrived at Grand Bayou. She couldn't explain it, deep down she was intrigued, and secretly desired to be part of a nontraditional religion.

"He didn't have to use magic, all he did was to give me the best fuck I ever had," Elizabeth revealed.

This revelation sent Binta into a violent rage, she grabbed Sinclare's wooden staff from its stand near the door, and swung, the tip caught Elizabeth on the side of the head causing semi loss of consciousness.

Elizabeth regained limited conscious when she struck the floor, face first. Binta moved quickly, she was on top of Elizabeth pressing the staff down on her neck before Elizabeth could react.

"Demon spirits leave this woman," she repeated over-and-over as she pressed down harder.

Elizabeth's brain was been starved of oxygen, she was losing conscious as she attempted to fight back.

Suddenly, the door to the cabin swung open with a violent blow as the wind rushed in knocking Binta backward.

The shattering of glass could be heard as the windows gave way under pressure as the tornado briefly touched ground and was quickly gone.

Elizabeth coughing, and breathing deep, stood up with hands on knees, looked into Binta's, who was still lying on the floor, raged filled eyes that matched her own.

The rage in both women eyes was soon replaced by a since of wonderment, they looked around the cabin disbelieving what they had just witnessed.

"What just happened?" Elizabeth asked

VII

After his meeting, with Susan Johnson, Nick wanted to know more about Leroy 'Silky' Anderson and his associates.

He had a lead on someone who may have been involve in Christina's disappearance, unless something else comes up this was the avenue he was going to pursue.

Angela Signorelli, a French-Canadian, and one of 'Silky' Anderson ladies, revealed, to Detective McCoy at NODP headquarter, that 'Silky' was heavily involved with the Voodoo community in

New Orleans and he was at Bayou St John the night of his death, because a secret ceremony took place.

Angela was not able to provide Detective McCoy with details about the ceremony, but she was able to provide a name, Julien Sinclare.

Detective McCoy drove out to Grand Bayou Plantation in an unsuccessful attempt to interview Sinclare, who was, at the time of the detective's visit, in his cabin with Elizabeth.

He did manager to speak with one of the other women that live at the plantation; Gloria, a voluptuous Cajun, whose breasts became his focus point, and an ally of Elizabeth.

He came away from Grand Bayou with more questions than answers, he noted in his report of the need to interview Sinclare.

***

Nick noticed the fear in the eyes of Angela Signorelli, who was sitting quietly at the table with only one of the Frank's, when he entered the office at Razzo Bar & Bistro.

Angela had been picked up on orders from the Frank's when they was giving the scoop, from Detective Forester, on the information she provided the NOPD on 'Silky' Anderson. Nick, giving the heads-up by one of the Frank's, came to talk to her.

Angela told Nick what she told the police about the night 'Silky' was at Bayou St John. "How close was 'Silky' to Julien Sinclare?" Nick asked.

"Nothing goes on without Sinclare known about it, but I don't think 'Silky' knew him personally," Angela answered.

"Who did he go to for advice or when he wanted herd remedies, that sort of thing?" Nick.

"He would always go to Lady Binta for everything," Angela answered sarcastically.

"What can you tell me about her?" Nick

"She scares me; I think she's been touched. She runs a palm reading and tarot cards business," Angela.

Nick sit-up when he heard Angela mention Binta's business, he recalled seeing the neon sign, Lady Binta's Palm Reading & Tarot Cards', near the International Hostel.

He placed the photograph of Christina on the table in front of Angela. "Have you seen her," Nick asked pointing to the photo.

Angela looked at the photo than shifted nervously in her chair, she looked at Nick then she turned and looked into the eyes of the one Frank; she began to sweat.

"Yes," she finally answered.
"Where," Nick demanded.
"She's at the house."

***

Silky had slipped the desk clerk at the International Hostel fifty dollars to point out the person who was putting up Elizabeth's photograph.

It was late in the evening, the hostel staff was about to change shifts when Antonio and Christina came through the front entrance, the desk clerk nodded towards them as they passed thru the lobby. Silky notice the clerk's nod and followed Antonio and Christina into the elevator.

Standing close, he saw Christina's potentials for earning money, and he wanted her.

***

After the incident, in Sinclare's cabin, Binta reevaluated her approach of bring Elizabeth back under her control.

She recalled her childhood experiences, in her village, Zooti, listening to the elders speak about courageous warriors, and appeasing of the spirits with blood rituals.

For hundreds of years the ancestors conducted these rituals with human sacrifices.

Binta had convinced herself that Sinclare has used powerful magic, and Elizabeth was not aware that he was controlling her thoughts.

She decided that she would need to evoke the ancient ancestral spirits to combat his powers. This would call for the sacrifice of blood; human blood.

Binta was kelp informed about the movement, and activities, of Antonio and Christina by 'Silky', and other informants.

It wasn't until she was provided a photograph, of the two visitors, that her mind reasoned that a person of Elizabeth's bloodline would be a powerful sacrifice.

She also surmised that this ritual would solidify her position with or without Sinclare's blessing.

Together with 'Silky', Binta hatched a plan to adduct Christina for the purpose of appeasing the ancestors.

The ceremony, to be led by Lady Binta, was passed by word of mouth to a small select number of loyal believers.

VIII

Binta was standing in the glow of the bonfire, naked, with arms outstretched, the heart of the young woman in one hand, and the sacrificial knife, dripping blood, in the other.

The people surrounding her, possessed by spirits, were all engaged in fornication when Sinclare, Gloria, and Elizabeth arrived at Bayou St John.

The three had just learned of Binta's intentions to perform a human sacrifice; rushed to try to stop the ritual.

The scene, spiritually intoxicating, drew Elizabeth and Gloria in; they started moving in tune with the drums, provocatively dancing together.

Sinclare, not affected by the spirits, was angry that Binta would try something like this without his guidance. He rushed forward, stood behind Binta who turned to face him.

He than took hold of the knife forcing it out of her hand, and forcing her to drop the heart to the ground.

"Spirits of the ancestors leave this place, you have been deceived," Sinclare repeated, in a strong booming voice that seems to descend from heaven.

The drums stopped abruptly, the atmosphere of the ceremony changed as the people's intoxication was replaced by the sobering reality, of the moment, sort to hide their nakedness.

In her madness Binta rushed towards Sinclare, Silky saw Binta's intentions; moved to stop her. The dart, laced with snake venom, found its mark in Silky's arm as he grabbed hold of Binta.

Sinclare rushed over, and scooped her up into his powerful arms, Binta, still adorning the mask of Lya Lase, went limp in his grasp.

"Worshippers of the spirits you have honored the ancestors and they are pleased", the voice of Elizabeth shouted over the noise of the crowd.

"Who are you? And how would you know?" the voice from the crowd shouted back.

"I am Elizabeth."

Mumbles went through the crowd, "the high priestess," she heard someone whisper.

"Acolyte," she continued, "to this woman," pointing to Binta.

"Take this body," Elizabeth pointed to the dead young woman, "bury her in the swamps and never speak of her again," she ordered.

Without question the body was whisked away.

"Go from this place, and rejoice in the experience," Elizabeth commanded.

She took the gris-gris and chicken foot from Sinclare's pocket, pinned it against the tree. As the people were leaving, each person touched the gris-gris, swearing their allegiance to Lady Binta.

No one noticed 'Silky' lying on the ground yards away.

***

"You said that you saw this woman at a house?" Nick asked Angela again.

"Yes," she repeated her answer.

"What house? Nick.

"Silky has a house on Urquhart Street, in the Ninth Ward, where he keeps new girls there before turning them out," Angela.

"And she's there now?" Nick asked, pointing to Christina's picture.

"She was yesterday, it's been days since anyone seen 'Silky', they could have scattered. She's in need of a fix about now."

"A fix, what do you mean?" the question came from the other side of the table, Frank leaned in.

Leroy 'Silky' Anderson was a pimp and hustler at heart, he followed the plan he and Binta had discussed. He adducted Christina by luring her into his car after she left the Café Armanda, for weeks he kept her in a zombified state with drugs provided him by Binta.

Been the hustler, he decided that Christina's value to his business out weighed his loyalty to the plan. He began to substitute Binta's drug with small amount of heroin. When Christina's cravings over took her will, 'Silky' would demand payment in the form of oral sex.

At first she would refuse, citing her Christian beliefs, and the fact that she was still a virgin. But the craving for heroin and his persistence finally chipped away her opposition. He would make her watch as other women would perform oral sex on him, then motion for her to follow suit, after awhile the heroin cravings alone was enough to motivate her.

Before he could turn Christina out, Binta had finalized her plans for the ceremony and wanted 'Silky' to get her ready. He wasn't about to give up this potential cash-cow.

He picked up a street junkie that resembled Christina, feed her the drug that Binta had prepared for Christina, took, and laid her on the sacrificial altar at Bayou St John.

***

"That's how he does it. Picks up young vulnerable women, usually runaways, gets them hooked on smack, make himself their god, and turns them out," Angela explained.

"Is that what happened to you?" Nick asked.

"No need, I was in the business before I met him," Angela.

"Had he turned Christina out?"

"Not yet".

A little over an hour later Detective Forester and Nick walked into the house on Urquhart Street in New Orleans Ninth Ward, after the uniformed police used a battering ram on the front door, and rounded up everyone inside.

Three women, dressed in lingerie, each displaying signs of heroin withdrawal symptoms, were sitting on the couch, guarded by a uniformed cop, when they entered.

Nick immediately recognized Christina; he pointed her out to Detective Forester.

"Christina Randazo," Detective Forester questioned.

The heroin fogged brain of Christina struggled with the ideal that the cop had called her name.

"How do you know me?" she asked.

"Christina Randazo, from Levanzo, Sicily?"

"Yes, but", Christina's mind finally grasped the reality of the situation. She knew at that moment that she had been rescued from her captivity. Tears clouded her eyes and ran down her cheeks.

She blessed herself with the sign of the cross and gave thanks to god.

****

Nick was happy that Christina, who was now in police custody, had survived her ordeal and was expected to make a good recovery.

He had telephoned Antonio in Rome, and was assured that Carmella would come to bring Christina home.

Now he would shift his focus on the difficult task of tracking Elizabeth.

VIX

Elizabeth and Sinclare sit cross-legged on the floor of Sinclare's cabin, Binta laid, legs tucked to her chest, on the floor babbling incomprehensibly. A sketched, written in white chalk, image of a Triskelion within a Circle encircled her body.

"What's wrong with her?" Elizabeth.

"She is been possessed by a vengeful spirit. We have to help her drive the spirit out, and than help her find her way back," Sinclare conjectured.

He rose from his position, walked over to the stone oven, took hold of a sage plant, and lit it. Walking from corner-to-corner, He allowed the smoke from the plant to fill each corner, while invoking the name of Lya Lase.

With thick smoke, and the smell of sage filling the room He put the burning plant back in the stone oven than sit down across from Elizabeth with Binta lying between them.

"Spirit that possesses this woman, reveal yourself," he repeated, over and over. His vocal rhythms take on a continuous chant.

Binta slowly sit-up, turned her head, it was not the voice of Sinclare that she responded to, but the voice of Elizabeth, who had began to chant the Swazi Sangoma praying-chant.

Binta stared at Elizabeth, as she continued the chant, with glazed eyes.

Binta got onto her knees, crawled over to Elizabeth, and glared into her eyes, their faces only inches apart.

"Where is Delta?" The voice came from Binta's mouth, but it was not hers.

"Where is Delta?" the voice asked again, directing the question to Elizabeth.

"Who is Delta, and what's your name?" Sinclare asked.

Ignoring Sinclare's question Binta shifted her head from side to side.

"You chant Delta's prayer, but you are not her. Where is Delta?" the voice, speaking inches from Elizabeth's face.

"Delta is with the ancestors, along time ago," Elizabeth.

"That I know. Where is she?"

"I don't understand," Elizabeth.

"You chant her prayer. She had to teach you. Where is Delta?"

"What is your name? And, why have you possessed this woman?" Sinclare tried again.

"This woman has to answer for her deception. Tell the witchdoctor to be quieted," the voice directed her response to Elizabeth.

Elizabeth glanced, peering over Binta's head, at Sinclare before responding.

"Delta did not teach me. I learned from her voice that was recorded long ago."

"Do you know its meaning?"

"No. Will you tell me?" Elizabeth.

"It is a prayer to easy the suffering of a people. It guides the souls of the tormented," the voice explained.

The room went silent. Sinclare was fascinated with this encounter and a little envious. "What deception do you speak of?" he demanded of the spirit.

Binta abruptly turned away from Elizabeth and faced Sinclare, who stared stoned-face at her.

"My name, witchdoctor, is not important. This woman tried to deceive the spirits with her offering," the voice.

"You are vengeful because of her offering? Leave this woman; Now!" he spoke in a powerfully commanding tone.

"The offering was unclean, and it had a non-repenting soul."

"Leave this woman," Sinclare commanded as he reached out, grabbed Binta by both shoulders, and pulled her into his arms.

Suddenly, a gust for wind blow, momentarily cleaning the heavy smoke from the sage plant, thru the room sending a cool breeze across Elizabeth's face. The essence of the spirit was on longer present after the breeze calmed.

"Damballah-Wado forgive me," Binta cried out.

Sinclare and Elizabeth looked at each other, than they each looked at Binta and then at each other again, both in disbelief. Binta's normally black hair now contained streaks of gray.

***

"Joseph Ranadzo," Joseph introduced himself, grasping Nick's hand in a firm handshake.

"Cleo Nickelson," Nick said his full name, following Joseph's lead, as he stood in the doorway of Carmella's suite at the Embassy Suites at the New Orleans International Airport.

"Mr. Nickelson please come-in." Carmella spoke from inside the suite.

Nick walked pass Joseph, who was blocking part of the doorway, Nick could smell the lingering scotch on his breath, and entered the room.

Carmella was sitting on the sofa, with Christina's head resting on her lap; she was stroking Christina's hair with her fingers.

"How's she doing?" Nick inquired.

"It will take time but she will recover. We obtaining drugs that will help to control the cravings, Detective Forester informed us that you were a big help in the rescue," Carmella voiced her gratitude.

Nick's mind couldn't help thinking that the road to recovery would be a long one for her, but his eyes was on the guy standing behind, and just to the right, of Carmella.

Bruno is an associate of the Palermo family, his primary function on this trip is to ensure nothing happens to Carmella.

"Thanks for coming," Carmella.

"No problem. There's nothing new on Elizabeth's whereabouts," Nick.

"But you do think that there is a connection between the people who adducted Christina and Elizabeth's disappearance?" Joseph asked.

"There is a possible connection that I will pursue, yes," Nick.

"I will be coming with you," Joseph announced.

"Mr. Nickelson"

"Nick," Nick interjected, responding to Carmella's formal address.

"It would be a great comfort to the family if you would allow Joseph to help,"

Carmella's request came in the form of a matter-of-fact statement, rather than a request.

"As you wish." Nick wasn't sure how helpful Joseph could be, but he didn't want to waste time objecting.

"We will be taking Christina back to Levanzo as soon as the authorities clear us," Carmella informed Nick.

Nick had the feeling that he had just been dismissed; he turned towards the door and walked out; followed closely behind by Joseph.

X

Rome is a place of mystery and discovery for a child whose imagination is larger than its young brain's ability to process all the stimuli vying for attention.

Elizabeth's imagination, along with her quizzical nature, was a constant topic of conversation among the adults in her family.

Each person who found themselves engaged with her was subjected to a barrage of questions on any topic that occupied her imagination at the time.

For most of Elizabeth's childhood, she and Joseph would attend mass at least twice per week, unlike her brother she never saw the church as a place of salvation for the soul or spiritual enlightenment, and she focused on the contradictions.

***

"Blessed be the god and father of our lord Jesus Christ, who according to his abundant mercy has begotten us again to a living hope through the resurrection of Jesus Christ from the dead," Father Paul, a young priest at the Church of Saint Mary of Jesus at the time, was quoting from The First Epistle of Peter.

Elizabeth, who loved to spend part of the summer in Levanzo with Christina and her family, giggled loudly, Christina elbowed her in the side, when Father Paul spoke of "receiving the end of your faith, the salvation of your souls". The words engendered quizzical skepticism in her mind, she thought about the rumored devil-worshipping at St Peter's in Rome.

The two girls, both practical jokers, spent the remainder of the service sitting in the second pew, behind an elderly couple, making funny faces at the altar boys.

***

"Hurry," Elizabeth shouted, her heart pounding in her chest, breathing heavy, she ran as fast as her legs could move. Her friends, laughing, was running behind her racing through the cemetery jumping over head stones as the security guard chased after the young teens.

One of the favorite pastimes for the group of friends was to write graffiti on the walls of tombs, and tormenting the cemeteries security.

These delinquent behaviors were a source of contention between Elizabeth and her father.

Antonio Randazo could not understand why his family principles and decorum had never been embraced by his, one and only, daughter.

"Elizabeth, where have I failed? You continue to bring shame on this family. You are not a little girl anymore, these incidents must stop," Antonio lectured Elizabeth.

"Father I know that I am not a little girl", Elizabeth.

"Is that all you have to say?"

"There is nothing I can say, or do, that would please you, so what is the point,"

Years later, rebelling from what she considered the restrictive structure of her parents home, Elizabeth found herself wondering the streets of Paris, after running away and become one of the many street people in that city.

Tired and a little afraid Elizabeth took refuge at the Cathedral Basilica of St Denis, an Abbey church, in the commune of Saint-Denis on the second night alone in Paris. She was having second thoughts about her decision to leave Rome.

Saint-Denis, a northern suburb of Paris, infamous in Paris for its high crime rates, is home to a small number of immigrants, not having French citizenship, from other countries. A few of these immigrants have managed to survive as part of the subculture in Paris.

"Hi, I'm Seth"

Elizabeth was laying on her back in the grass, on the lawn of the Cathedral, deep in thought, she had decided to go back to Rome, she haven't decided when, when the sound of Seth's voice made her look up, the sun was shining bright, she had to shield her eye from the glare in order to see who had spoken.

Seth stood over Elizabeth smiling down at her. "I'm Seth," he spoke again as he extended his hand.

"Elizabeth," she responded, extending her hand up to shake his.

"You looked like you were miles away," Seth.

"I was," Elizabeth agreed.

Seth, a flamboyant leader of one of the groups that survives in the shadow of French society, has a toxic personality. His ability to draw people to him has been will crafted. He engaged Elizabeth in conversation for over an hour, at the end she was captivated by his world view.

She became involved with a group that believed in Nordic Racial Paganism and whom had a strong belief in Animism, belief that souls and spirits exist not only in humans but also in other animals, plants, rocks, and natural phenomena.

Seth, been the leader of this group, would often quote from the book 'The call of Our Ancient

Nordic Religion' by Alexander Mills who believed that Nordic Racial Paganism was, "spiritual rediscovery of the Aryan ancestral gods intended to embed the white races in a sacred worldview that supports their tribal feeling".

Elizabeth was indoctrinated in this belief, that professed faith in a number of gods and goddesses, system until she grew tried of the dogma that left her longing for something else.

After a year, of living hand-to-mouth on the streets of Paris, she returned to Rome determined to make a mend with her parents and make a fresh start.

Joseph was the one person happiest to see her return, he had under a year left at the University, but that did not keep him from visiting with Elizabeth on weekends. During one such visit they made plans to travel across America.

***

The events of the last few weeks saw a change come over Binta, she became more reflective, and, to some, her demeanor mirrored that of Sinclare's. For a period of time whenever Sinclare would mediate or consult with the ancestors Binta would be by his side.

Elizabeth was left to see after the needs of the people who came to the plantation seeking a meeting with Lady Binta. Elizabeth's reputation for been knowledgeable had been growing, every since she aided Thomas, made it easier for her to gain the trust of the people.

Those seeking amulets for protection against harm, or potions to attract love, insisted on Lady Binta involvement. During these occasions Binta never spoke, Elizabeth communicated any information that needed to be shared.

***

The darkest of night was intruded upon by a flash of bright electrifying lighten, moments later, rolling thunder shook the ground with a loud explosion. A continuous down pour of rain beat upon the roof making its presence known.

Elizabeth sat cross-legged in the middle of her bed listening to the water ran down the gutter in tune with the rain gathering in large puddles out side her window. It was past mid-night, she hadn't been able to sleep, conflicting emotions had been causing her an unusually amount of stress.

The major cause of her turmoil was the conflict between her Catholic upbringings, which has began to become constant in her thoughts, and that of spirit worshipping of which Voodoo in based upon.

With her arms hanging relaxed along her side, the back of her hand rested gently on her knees with thumbs and forefingers touching, her back straight, breathing deep taking air into her nose and exhaling through her mouth.

She closed her eyes, attempting to empty her mind of thought, trying not to think of the battle that rage in her conscious. She would allow the different conflicts to work out solutions using her other senses.

Tingles of emotions cascaded through her causing her body to shiver. She was there again, the serpent draped around her, dancing with Binta the night that she was counted among the believers.

She recalled the feeling as she moving to the beat of the drums. The sound was part of her, she was the rhythm, and her hips swayed from side to side as the crown danced in tune with her movement.

Sinclare's touch sent a fury of ecstasy through her as her feet was lifted off the ground. He cradled her in his arms. The strong odor of his musk penetrated her nostrils causing intoxication.

No satisfactory outcome to the conflicts between her Catholic upbringing and her adopted belief in spirit worshipping was achieved. Affirmation as to why she wanted to remain at Grand Bayou Plantation eased some of the tension.

She smiled, "Sinclare."

XI

Sinclare, not fazed by Detective McCoy's harsh questions, sat expressionless looking down at the photograph of Leroy 'Silky' Anderson. Detective McCoy sat across, on the other side of the table, eyeing Sinclare suspiciously.

The Detective, determined to find out what Sinclare knew about what went on at Bayou St John's, made another trip out to Grand Bayou Plantation but he was again unsuccessful at interviewing Sinclare. It was Gloria who relayed Detective

McCoy's request, that Sinclare contact him as soon as possible, to Sinclare when he returned to the Plantation.

Sinclare decided to go to the NOPD Homicide Division to talk with the Detective in person.

"Mr. Anderson was found dead at Bayou St John. I was hoping that you could help me determine what happened," Detective McCoy said, placing his finger on the photograph.

"I don't know how I can help you since I don't know this person," Sinclare said questioningly.

"Yes, I'm sure that you and the victim weren't acquainted."

"So why did you want to speak to me?"

"What can you tell me about a Voodoo ritual that took place at Bayou St John a few weeks ago?"

"Why do you think that I would have knowledge of a ritual?" Sinclare.

"Mr. Sinclare you must know that since Mr. Anderson's body was found we have gathered pieces of evidences. We have also interviewed a number of persons that speaks highly of you, which lead me to believe that nothing happens in the Parishes without your knowledge," Detective McCoy.

"You give me too much credit. I do not know of a ritual. Why are you trying to link me with this death?"

The image of 'Silky' on the photograph did not register with Sinclare until Detective McCoy mentioned Bayou St John, then he recognized 'Silky' as the person who had intervened, grabbing Binta when she lunged towards him. He had no plans of volunteering this information.

"Why don't you tell me what happened at Bayou St John", Detective McCoy spoke in a stringent tone.

At the time Detective McCoy was interviewing Sinclare, Nick received a telephone call from

Delon Pierre at the Café Armanda requesting that he come to the restaurant. He informed Nick that he may have information that would be of interest.

"I'm sorry Detective but I can not help you," Sinclare declared as he stood to leave.

"What can you tell me about Lady Binta?" Detective McCoy asked, standing between Sinclair and the door.

"We share the same residence. But you already know this."

"Yes, yes. Did you know that Lady Binta and the dead guy were close friends?"

"No I didn't, I'm sure she has a lot of friends that I am not aware of".

"Yes I'm sure. There's no reason for you to leave town is there? I may need to speak with you again," Detective McCoy said confidently as he moved aside to allow Sinclare to leave.

***

In the early hours of the following morning, while it was still dark outside, Sinclare laid awake on his makeshift bed reconfirming his next move in dealing with Detective McCoy when the door to his cabin opened slightly, a figure slid thru the opening.

From the gentle glow from the lantern he could see that it was Elizabeth.
She walked over and straddled him, legs on each side of him, looking down at him with wild passion in her eyes, she was naked, and her hair flowed down to middle of her back.

She reached down and moved the covers to one side exposing Sinclare's male member. She grabbed hold of it, stroked until she knew it was ready, she eased herself down on top allowing it to penetrate her moist opening. A soft mourn escaped her lips as she slid Sinclare deeper inside.

He tried to sit up but she pushed him back down, she made it known that she was in control. Her hips moved up and down until she finally reached her peek. She collapsed on top of Sinclare and fell asleep listening to his heart beat.

Elizabeth was awakened by a gentle touch on her shoulder and the soft call of her name. She looked up into the eyes of Binta, and then looked around for Sinclare, he was not there. She gently rubbed her stomach; intuitively she knew that Sinclare seed had found its mark.

It wasn't long after that Binta felt sure that she had made amends for her errors at Bayou St John; now there was something else she wanted to correct.

The years since she arrived at Grand Bayou has pasted one by one, Elizabeth could barely recognize any other place in New Orleans outside the grounds of the plantation. It came as a surprise when Binta asked her to accompany her on a trip to the studio; she jumped at the chance.

Elizabeth glazed out the window, toes tipping to the sounds of music from the radio, as the long Lincoln Continental made its way over the Huey P. Long Bridge, and navigated the streets of the city to arrive at Binta's Palm Reading Studio.

Elizabeth recalled seeing the noon sign for the first time.

The two women was parked on the curve outside the studio, both captivated by that sight of the moon's bright illumination.

"I don't know where you came from that first night you showed up, but here is where you can leave, and go from where you came," Binta announced.

Elizabeth was speechless, tears dripped from the corner of her eyes. Looking up the street she knew that the International Hostel, the only other place of reference she had, was somewhere around the corner.

Binta had gotten out of the car and was entering the building when Elizabeth turned and looked at her; Binta briefly glanced back at her before closing the door behind her.

Elizabeth sit frozen in the moment, the image of her mother was in the forefront of her mind. She thought of the pain and hardship that her mother must have gone thru over the years of not knowing what had happened to her.

She blessed herself with the sign of the cross, something that she haven't done since she was a young child, and begun to wonder how she was going to explain the years that she was missing. How could she make her family understand? When she did not fully understand what kelp her from leaving Grand Bayou; before now.

A sudden shock of reality made her heart race, she placed her hand of her stomach and wondered how she was going to explain, if her intuitions was correct that Sinclare's seed had started life growing, her desire to have his child. Was Binta right all alone? Had Sinclare used magic to control her mind?

She wasn't sure of the answers but she was sure that she was not ready to face her father without knowing. She opened the door to the car, allowed her feet to touch ground; she stood watching the traffic flow up and down the street.

She closed the door behind her as she entered Binta's studio.

***

Nick and Joseph arrived at Café Armanda to meet with Delon Pierre during the afternoon hours. The restaurant was filled to capacity, the three men met in Delon's small cramped office.

"Look's like we came at a bad time," Nick.

"Yes, it's our busy time," Delon acknowledged.

"This," Nick turned towards Joseph, "is Joseph Randazo. He's the cousin of Christina, the young lady we spoke about, and who came in here. I am happy to say that Christina has been found alive."

"That's good news. According to Detective Forester there is another missing woman from the same family," Delon.

"Yes, my sister Elizabeth", Joseph interjected.

"Sorry to hear that. Have you heard of the Grand Bayou Plantation?" Delon addressed his question to Nick.

"No can't say I have."

"It's owned by Julien Sinclare."

"I have heard that name," Nick said excitedly.

"He is known around the Parishes as a Hoodoo Witchdoctor. He lives with three women who is said to be his wives."

"Witchdoctor?" Joseph blared out his disbelief.

"They do exist," Delon.

"You think that Sinclare has something to do with Elizabeth's disappearance?" Nick inquired.

"Talk of a fourth woman living at the plantation. People are referring to her as the High Priestess, they say that she is acolyte to Lady Binta, one of Sinclare's wives, and to most in the Parishes the Queen of Voodoo", Delon.

"That's another name I have came across," Nick.

"This fourth woman is said to be called Elizabeth."

"What can you tell us about Sinclare?" Nick.

"You could not miss him; he's a really large man with dark skin. Have a lot of tattoos that you can barely see on his dark skin. When he talks he can captivate you with his deep booming voice. But what makes Sinclare special is his extraordinary ability to use mind control on believers."

"What do you mean about believers and is he dangerous?" Joseph.

"I would suggest that he is as dangerous as anyone who holds the aspirations of a religion and can get other to act on the behalf of that religion. Believers in this instants are those that believe in Voodoo," Delon.

"Have you told Detective Forester this information?" Nick.

"Not yet, you got here before him. I expect that he will be coming this evening."

Nick and Joseph left the Café Armanda, drove to the corner of River Road and Ormond Blvd where Nick placed a call to Detective Forester.

"We are going to that plantation?" Joseph questioned. He was anxious, ready to charge off and confront Sinclare.

"Not yet, we will let the police take the lead."

***

Detective Forester was waiting at Razzo Bar & Bistro when Nick and Joseph arrived. "Ha! Mr. PI," one of the Frank's called out from behind the bar. "What you having?"

"Two, scotch-n-water," Nick ordered for himself, and Joseph, then walked over and joined Detective Forester at his table.

"Detective I think you already know Joseph," Nick.

Detective Forester did not respond to Nick, he eyed Joseph with outwardly show of distaste.

It was now late in the day, there was only a few tables occupied, the one Frank was busy restocking liquor behind the bar, Frank Sinatra's voice was coming from the jukebox, which always seems to be the case when Nick came into the Bistro.

The smell of garlic and baked bread from the kitchen made Joseph's stomach growl from hunger, he when to the bar to retrieve the two drinks before taking a sit at the table.

"Like I said over the phone we met with Mr. Pierre at the Café Armanda, he gave us a possible lead on Elizabeth. We need to check out the Grand Bayou Plantation," Nick informed the Detective.

"The Grand Bayou Plantation?" Detective Forester questioned.

"Yes. You've heard of it?" Nick.

"It's out in the Parishes; nothing ever goes on out there." Detective Forester couldn't think of a time when NOPD had to go out to the plantation.

"What makes Mr. Pierre think that this Elizabeth is the missing woman?" Detective Forester.

"He couldn't say that she is the same woman. But there is a mystery as to where she came from, the fact that she is a young white woman makes it highly possible," Nick.

"Ok, I will get a judge to sign off on a search warrant. You can ride along tomorrow," Detective Forester.

"Tomorrow?" "Let's go now," Joseph demanded.

"I think that it would be best if you leave Mr. Randazo behind," the detective addressed Nick, without responding to Joseph's demand.

"I'm going," Joseph shouted. He was feeling disrespected by Detective Forester and he were emboldened by the scotch.

Detective Forester, red-faced by indignation, squared his shoulders and locked his focus on Joseph, "Mr. Randazo this is now a police matter. If you interfere I will not hesitate in arresting you. Do you understand?"

"Detective Forester I will have to agree with Joseph on this. We should check out this plantation today," Nick intervened, noticing that the tension between the two men was escalating to a boiling point.

"Tomorrow will be soon enough, I will need a warrant"

"I will not wait, if my sister is at that plantation I will find her. So detective go get your warrant, I don't need one."

***

Marvin Espinoza, a bus boy at the Café Armanda, is a frequent visitor at the Grand Bayou Plantation, and he is a zealous practitioner of the Voodoo religion.

As a loyal devotee to Lady Binta, Marvin is one of many who will willingly lay down their life's to shield her from danger, was on the telephone, after over hearing the conversation coming from Delon's office, immediately after Nick and Joseph left the Café.

***

Nick got up from the table, went into the office to speak with the one Frank, who gave him directions to Grand Bayou; he also placed a .38 caliber revolver into Nick's hand. Nick tucked the pistol into his waist under his shirt, gave Frank a nod, and walked out. Joseph was already outside, on Bourbon Street, waiting.

The drive to the Grand Bayou Plantation was not a peaceful one for Nick, Joseph raged on and on against Detective Forester.

It was dark with calm skies, a full bright moon illuminating the road when Nick turned onto the one leading up to the main house. Cars lined one side of the road protected by a canopy of branches from the oak trees that line both sides.

The sound of jazz blared over the sound of laughter and chatter of the people inside. The party was hastily put together by Gloria, after the telephone call from Marvin, in anticipation of a visit from the NOPD, was attended by close associates and friends of Grand Bayou.

Gloria also used the party as an opportunity to remove all signs that Elizabeth had ever been at the plantation.

Nick and Joseph sit listening and watching the house for a period of time.

"Let's go," Nick finally said.

Sinclare was meeting with a small number of prominent members of New Orleans business community. Not only is Sinclare shrewd and conning as a leader within the Voodoo community, he is also known to be ruthless in business.

Over the years he has managed to strong-arm his way into a number of partnerships in a variety of ventures, mostly small well established businesses throughout the Lower Ninth Wards.

The meeting was interrupted by Joanne, the third of Sinclare's reported wives. She handed him a business card, written in Italian, and told him that a private detective from Rome was asking to speak to him. Sinclare looked at the card than handed it back to Joanne, who took the card and left the room.

"I'm sorry but Sinclare is not able to speak with you today. But if you leave the number to where you are staying he will call you when he's available," Joanne informed Nick, who was still standing outside on the porch.

"Maybe you can allow us to speak with Elizabeth," Joseph asked.

"There's no Elizabeth here. I must get back to my guess, Sinclare will get in touch with you," Joanne insisted, closing the door on the two men.

Joseph pushed the door open and stepped into the house and was immediately confronted by two large men, each dressed in two piece African dashiki attire, who forced him back out onto the porch then ordered the two men to leave the property.

Nick was angry, Joseph's boneheaded move and his lack of rational thinking was hindering his efforts.

On the way back to the car he wrote down some of the license plates numbers, he was thinking of ways to get around the roadblocks that will surely go up to protect Sinclare after this incident.

"Joseph if you want the help your sister you must avoid this type of outburst," Nick said as he drove away from Grand Bayou.

"I think that she was lying about Elizabeth," Joseph.

"Maybe so, but we will never find out now," Nick.

***

Delon Pierre was making final adjustments to his purchase order, before closing for the night, when an urgent knock on the door to the Café interrupted his focus.

He got up from his desk and walk out into the café, looked out through the glass of the front door into the face of Marcel Jean-Baptiste, an Haitian enforcer for one of the Lower Ninth Ward's drug dealer, and a personal friend of Julien Sinclare.

"Sorry sir, we are closed", Delon shouted through the door.

"Yes, I know sir but it is important that I speak to you," Marcel shouted back in response.

Delon hadn't wanted to open the door; he felt that something wasn't right. He walked slowly to the door keeping his eye on Marcel as he moved forward.

"What does it concerns?" Delon.

"It's about your wife, Cheryl," Delon heard Marcel say.

He spied at Marcel for what seem to be a full minute before opening the door and allowed his visitor to past through.

Delon push the door and heard it slam shut, he felt the pistol poke his side before seeing it.

Marcel had removed a .45cal Smith & Western from his waist and pushed it into Delon's side, in one swift experienced motion, before Delon could react.

"In the back," Marcel ordered.

XII

Detective Forester and a team of officers arrived at Grand Bayou with a search warrant, all of the residents except Binta and Elizabeth was present.

"You all have a sit in the living room and allow my officers to do their job," Detective Forester said after placing the warrant in Sinclare's hand.

"Which one of you women is Lady Binta?" the Detective asked.

"Nether, she's out," Sinclare answered.

"Where can I find her? I need to speak to her."

"I will pass your request along," Sinclare.

"How about Elizabeth, is she here?"

"Detective no one name Elizabeth lives here," Sinclare spoke forcefully.

"You do understand that we are investigating a crime? If you hinder my efforts you will be arrested," Detective Forester turned away and walked into the den.

After a thorough search no evidence of Elizabeth was found. He drove away from Grand Bayou frustrated and disappointed. He decided to make the trip over to the Café Armanda to speak with Delon Pierre.

***

Binta and Elizabeth spent the night, and most of the following day, at the studio talking, and experimenting with a variety of herbal remedies.

Elizabeth decide that time was not right for her to leave Grand Bayou, when Binta closed the studio Elizabeth was with her as she navigated the streets for the drive back to the plantation.

Nick and Joseph turned the corner off Carondelet Street and walked the few blocks towards the neon sign as Binta drove away; Nick had convinced Joseph that they should check out Lady Binta's Palm Reading.

The studio was closed when they arrived, Nick made quick work at picking the lock, and the two entered the studio.

***

Nether of the women knew of the activities that had taking place at the house, Gloria was there when they returned and had to brief Binta.

Elizabeth listened carefully and was shocked to here that a private detective from Rome had been at the house.

Immediately she thought of her father, he was not the kind of man that would give up on his family. The other surprise came when Gloria described the man that accompanies the detective, "Joseph" she said.

The two women turned and looked at her. "The person you described could have been my brother Joseph," Elizabeth explained.

"The men are staying at the International Hostel over on Carondelet Street. Here's the number," Gloria handed the information to Binta.

Elizabeth and Binta looked at each other knowing that they had just left that area, and that Elizabeth chooses not to walk away.

***

Detective Forester arrived at Café Armanda to find the New Orleans Crime Scene Investigation Unit at the restaurant. Delon Pierre was found dead of apparent strangulation earlier that morning, Detective McCoy was assign lead investigator.

"Hi Mac", Detective Forester called out as he approached the scene.

"Robert, what are you during here?" Detective McCoy questioned.

"I was on my way here to speak to the manager, Mr. Pierre."

"Sorry you're too late; he was found dead this morning."

"How did it happen?"

"Look's like he was strangled. What business did you have with Mr. Pierre?" Detective McCoy.

"He asked me to come. Reportedly he had information on one of my open missing person cases, you remember the missing female from Rome a few years ago," Detective Forester.

"Yes, I remember that our paths crossed once before in relation to that case. I still have an open case that links to 'Silky' Anderson, who was linked to a Lady Binta."

"This all couldn't be coincidental. Mr. Pierre suppose to have information about a new resident at the Grand Bayou Plantation, people say that her name is Elizabeth. The Grand Bayou is the home of Lady Binta and Julien Sinclare, two persons of interest," Detective Forester briefed.

"Yes, I know. Have you been out there? I interviewed Mr. Sinclare at the station, couldn't pin him down on what happened at Bayou St John's but I thank he knows something?"

"Yes, just executed a search warrant. Found nothing."

"Let's share notes on this one, our cases appears to overlap," Detective McCoy suggested, he was thinking of bring all the residents of Grand Bayou in for questioning.

"That sounds good. See you back at headquarters," Detective Forester spoke walking towards his vehicle.

***

Like Marie Laveau before her, Binta is a devoted Catholic who incorporates elements of Catholicism into her practice of Voodoo.

Joseph was taking aback by some of the paraphernalia in Binta's studio. One item seems to disturb him the most was a carving of a crucifix intertwined by a serpent that is displayed on a small altar.

"Blasphemy," Joseph muttered.

Nick dipped his figure into a pot filled with herbs and water, the water was lukewarm to the touch.

"Someone was here recently," he called out to Joseph.

"How can you tell?" Joseph asked as he came through the door to the kitchen.

"This water is still slightly warm."

The two men continue to search the studio, but nothing that indicates that Elizabeth had been there was found. Joseph was getting more-and-more frustrated, he sensed that this was a waste of time; he wanted to go back to Grand Bayou.

They left the kitchen, and went back into the studio, Nick's attention was drawn to a tiny chest lying next to the small altar, and he picked it up and opens the hinged top.

The photograph that Antonio Randazo had taped to the window of Binta's studio came in handed. She banded the photograph around the gris-gris she had made with strings of Elizabeth's hair and stuffed it into the chest then placed it next to the altar as a gift to Iwa Damballah Welo.

Finding the photo rapped around the doll gave conformation, for Joseph, that there was a connection between Lady Binta and Elizabeth's disappearance, Nick wondered about its meaning.

It was dark out when to men walk out of Lady Binta's Palm Reading & Tarot Cards. Nick stuffed the chest under his arm as they turned onto Carondelet Street in the direction of the International Hostel.

Detective Forester, who was sitting in his car outside the hostel, yelled out Nick's name when he saw the men approaching.

***

From the French Quarters, and Bourbon Street, to New Orleans downtown, to far out into the Parishes a light fog laid just above the ground of south Louisiana. Misty dew wet the grounds of

Grand Bayou Plantation as a heavier fog hovered overhead.

The five member residents was seated on the bare ground outside of Sinclare's cabin swaying to the beats arranged by the two drummers sitting off to the side.

The glow from the low fire was the only light that penetrated the darkness, with the sound of crickets chirruping in the distance along with the occasional howling from a lone coyote the only other sounds.

Sinclare, sitting cross-legged in the middle of the four women, had prepared a special tea whose effect had started to take effect. Sinclare called out for the spirits to come and rejoice.

Elizabeth was the first to feel the effects of the tea, her mind twirled out of control, she had to lay flat on her back to stop the dizziness, the other three women was been effected the same way.

In the darkness of each of the woman's mind a bright light shined in the distance, a figure appeared beckoning them to come. The soft sound of Sinclare's name escaped from the lips of the four women like a chorus. They each tried to reach out to him but the distance seemed too great, only the rhythm of the drums was heard in the silence of their minds causing their bodies to move erotically.

Detective Forester pulled his vehicle up to the front of the main house of Grand Bayou followed close behind by Nick and Joseph.

The four women was now feeling the full effect of the hallucinate drug in the tea, the distant light in their minds was shining brighter, the figure was getting closer. They each could see Sinclare's face but his body was that of a serpent, they gasped in unison at the sight.

Lady Binta, Gloria, and Joanne embraced the image; their movement became more and more erotic.

But, Elizabeth screamed out.

Detective Forester took his sidearm out of its holster, the three men ran in the direction of the scream, and the sound of the drums.

Coming upon the scene the men stopped short and viewed the spectacle that was taking place around the fire, in opened mouth suspense.

They saw four women lying on their backs, their bodies' movement emulating the movement of snakes, and Sinclare sitting on the ground between them.

"Freeze don't anyone move", Detective Forester shouted.

No one, outside the drummers who abruptly stop beating their drums, heard his command.

Sinclare was in a deep trance his mind and body separated, the four women was under the influence of hallucinogenic herbs their minds was been controlled by the spirit of Damballah.

Joseph recognizes Elizabeth immediately, rushed over to where she laid on the ground. He scooped her into his arms then sits down, and placed her head in his lap; calling out her name he sobbed.

The night was violently disturbed by the sound of an explosion, then the voice of pain echoed as the .38 caliber slug from Nick's gun penetrated Sinclare's chest just before the dagger in his hand could fine its mark in Joseph's back.

The spell of the night had been broken. The four women, shocked out of their hallucinations, became hysterical when they saw Sinclare lying on the ground with blood pulsing from his chest.

Joseph attempted to restrain Elizabeth but she broke from his grasp and crawled over to join the other three women who wailed in grieve next to Sinclare's body.

Nick and Detective Forester witnessed Elizabeth's reactions; the two men looked at each other both with questioning expressions, while Joseph looked on.

****

The small inland of Levanzo, Sicily, where a large portion of the people made their living from the sea as fishermen, or boat makers, proved to have the perfect climate to aid in the fight, and recovery, of heroin addition.

With the hardship of her experience in New Orleans behind her, Christina has been able to re-devote herself to her faith of Catholicism.

On this morning, Mass seems to carrier more meaning for Christina, she had been pacing all night, hyped with anticipation. The day that she has been hoping, and praying for has finally arrived.

Today, Elizabeth and her family will arrive from Rome, this will be the first time the two women has seen one another since their time together in New Orleans.

Elizabeth's return, which Antonio Randazo ordered be kelp among immediate family, was marked by periods of harsh adjustments. The Randazo's worked tirelessly to help Elizabeth gain strength to fight her internal battles.

The mysteries of her experience at Grand Bayou have yet to reveal themselves, and the struggle between her two faiths rages on.

The first person that Antonio called when he felt Elizabeth was making progress was his brother, Carlos, who demanded that they come to Levanzo.

"You must come," Carlos said.

Elizabeth has been looking forward to this day ever since her family decided to announce her return; it was the day that she would see Christina.

Christina was the first to see the car pull into the driveway, she ran out of the house when she saw Elizabeth get out of the car.

The two women embraced, sobbing joyfully.

Elizabeth and Christina walked arm-in-arm along the long pier as they had done many times as children.

The rows of fishing boats teetered banged against the pier as the oceans water splashed their hulls.

The crews, working in preparation to set sail the following morning, stopped momentarily to watch the women pass, most taking note of the one with the swollen stomach.

"How long, before the baby's due?" Christina asked.

"Any day now."

Reference:

Wikipedia, The Free Encyclopedia @ http://
en.wikipedia.org

New Orleans Paranormal & Occult Research Society Ghostly Gallery @ www.neworleansghosts.com

Major Arcana Tarot Cards

A Voice of Awareness

In order to obtain self-awareness one has to enter a process of change. One must look within for answers to life adjusting questions.

For we as humans need to recognize and embrace the Voice Of Awareness that is built into all human consciousness. We know that god has blessed the human species with the ability to reason.
Once you allow reason to guide your thought process you enter a new level of awareness that comes with a voice that speaks to the individual.

The first question one may ask when speaking of the Voice Of Awareness is where does this voice come from? Moreover, how does it communicate with the person?

Taking the first part of this question, I see two possible answers, 1- Physiological or 2- Emotional. In exploring the possible physiological answer one may ask, does this voice speak through the conscious or subconscious mind?
When looking at the second half of this

question one may ask, which of the many avenues of emotions does this voice use to communicate?

I believe that this Voice Of Awareness is subconsciously based that uses the conscious emotions of guilt and anger as a vehicle to communicate with the person.

The link of communication between the Voice Of Awareness and the person is accomplished in an adverse manner.

Learning to understand the language used by the Voice Of Awareness can be a life long process. It is my contention that all humans know when the Voice Of Awareness is speaking; the goal is to learn to listen.

I believe that when the Voice Of Awareness speaks to us through the use of guilt it causes emotional instability, physical illness, sleeplessness, and mental disorders.

Emotional instability includes such things as depression, sleeplessness, isolationism, loneliness, and empathy.

Physical illness includes ulcers; migraines, high blood pressure, and back pain.

Mental disorder includes phobia, and neurosis.

When the Voice Of Awareness speaks through the use of anger, we have a more volatile situation, which could lead to socially destructive behavior.

Anger is an emotion that is the most misunderstood emotion of all. Anger is useful in relieving the person of stress that may manifest itself into other mental, emotional, or physical conditions.

Anger in itself is not and has never been a negative emotion. Anger like all emotions brings about behavior.

This behavior is one of the ways, therein; the Voice Of Awareness uses to communicate with the person.

Reasoning is gods gift to the human species, to say that the Voice Of Awareness do not communicate in pleasurable ways is correct.

However, pleasure maybe achieved, by freeing the self of guilt and controlling ones behavior when angered. Gaining power over ones behavior puts the person squarely in control of ones destiny.

This freedom, itself, brings a deep pleasure within.

As one goes though this process of change one gains the ability to and is willing to listen to their internal awareness speak to the consciousness. It is like an awakening of a pattern of thought that one was not aware of before.

One can began to put life's events and the people that share those events into perspectives learned from listen to the Voice Of Awareness of self.

Making the transition from one stage of life to another one can only hope that the Voice Of Awareness will become clearer.

DARE, O! DARE
Go beyond your perceived limitations.